Murphy

Gold Rush Dog

Murphy

Gold Rush Dog

Written by Alison Hart

Illustrated by Michael G. Montgomery

PEACHTREE
PUBLISHERS

Published by
PEACHTREE PUBLISHERS
1700 Chattahoochee Avenue
Atlanta, Georgia 30318-2112
www.peachtree-online.com

Text © 2014 by Alison Hart
Illustrations © 2014 by Michael G. Montgomery

First trade paperback edition published in 2018

Cover illustration rendered in oil on canvas board; interior illustrations in pencil and
watercolor. Title, byline, and chapter headings typeset in Hoefler & Frere-Jones's Whitney
fonts by Tobias Frere-Jones; text typeset in Adobe's Garamond by Robert Slimbach.

Cover design by Nicola Simmonds Carmack
Book design by Melanie McMahon Ives

Printed in February 2018 in the United States of America by LSC Communications in
Harrisonburg, Virginia
10 9 8 7 6 5 4 3 2 1 (hardcover)
10 9 8 7 6 5 4 3 2 1 (trade paperback)

HC: 978-1-56145-769-4
PB: 978-1-68263-039-6

Library of Congress Cataloging-in-Publication Data

Hart, Alison, 1950-
Murphy, Gold Rush dog / by Alison Hart ; illustrated by Michael Montgomery.
pages cm
ISBN: 978-1-56145-769-4
Summary: "In 1900, a dog named Murphy wants to help Sally and Mama build a new life
in Nome, but life in the mining town is not easy. Can the three of them find a home—and
maybe a fortune?"— Provided by publisher. 1. Dogs—Juvenile fiction. [1. Dogs—Fiction.
2. Gold mines and mining—Fiction. 3. Nome (Alaska)—Gold discoveries—Fiction.] I.
Montgomery, Michael, 1952-
illustrator. II. Title.
PZ10.3.H247Mu 2014
[Fic]—dc23
                                    2013049354

To adventurous ladies past and present
—A. H.

CONTENTS

CHAPTER ONE

Carlick

June 5, 1900

Marche!" A whip stung my neck, but my legs were too weak to run any faster.

Old Blue led our team. Behind him, Cody and I trotted side-by-side, though Cody was starting to lag. Tooni, the Alaskan driver, jogged alongside us, panting as hard as we were. His snowshoes slapped against the crusted top layer of the snowy trail.

We were all bone-weary, but the man in the sledge again shouted for us to go faster. *Faster. Faster.* By now I hated that word and Carlick, the man who hollered it.

"Faster, you lazy beasts!" Carlick sat in the sledge, covered with skins, only his eyes visible beneath his fur cap.

Tooni's lash struck Cody, who yelped and fell. Slowing, Blue and I dragged him, my raw feet scrabbling at the snow. The harness bit into my aching shoulders where the leather had rubbed off my fur. Then Cody regained his footing, and we lurched forward again.

The ice cracked beneath my paws, and I smelled

water. A hole ahead. Blue veered right. I tugged left, hoping the sledge would plunge into the freezing Yukon, taking Carlick with it.

"Gee!" the driver ordered. "Gee, you cursed dogs!" He had also spotted the hole.

Blue followed the command and forced us to the right, away from the river and onto a packed trail already crowded with travelers. Another team of dogs floundered in a snowdrift, its driver flogging them. We passed a man perched on a strange two-wheeled thing. Other men pulled their sledges like animals. A snow-covered horse, its head hanging wearily, high-stepped around them. The rider on its back was as hunched as the horse.

"Faster!" Carlick hollered. "I must get to Nome to stake a gold claim before all these stampeders!"

Nome. Gold. Carlick had repeated these words each time we camped after leaving the place called Dawson City. As I ran along the frozen trail, my paws left bloody tracks. I hoped the words meant finding a home—and ending this terrible journey.

◁≋▷

"Tie Murphy tightly," Carlick told Tooni when we finally stopped.

Tooni reached for my harness. I growled and my hackles rose. I wanted to lunge at him, but the driver raised his whip and I cowered.

"He's learning who's master," Carlick said approvingly. "And he's still hearty after this hard trip." He glanced at Blue and Cody. "The other two are done for. Tomorrow, cut them loose. They can fend for themselves. I'll need Murphy to haul all my riches now that we're at Nome."

Tooni hammered a stake into the snowy earth and tied one end of a rope to it. He checked the other end, which was knotted to the leather collar around my neck.

Carlick returned to his cabin. When he opened the door, I could smell meat cooking inside. Cody and Blue whined hungrily. The driver threw us chunks of raw tomcod, then crawled into his tent. I gulped my fish down, bone and all.

When I was young I had known a gentle touch, a heaping bowl, and a loving home. Then I'd been sold to Carlick who needed a new dog for his sled team. He'd driven us hard. We'd traveled for days and days with no kind words, no warm straw bed, and not enough food to fill our stomachs. So far, this place called *Nome* was no better than the camps where we'd stayed on the way. And it was not a home.

The snow was belly deep. Blue was already curled up, licking the sores on his paws. He had taught me well on the trip, but now he was thin, his coat was ragged, and he'd limped the last miles. Cody was also exhausted and lame. Tucking their heads under their tails, they fell asleep.

The wind howled around us. I circled, trying to make a nest. My thick fur kept me warm, but I couldn't rest.

Dark closed in, and lights blinked in the distance.

Somewhere in this new place, there might be a home for me. I would never find my old littermates. They had long been scattered. But if I was to find a true home, I needed to get away from Carlick.

I gnawed on the rope. My teeth were strong and sharp, but the night was short. The sun would rise early. I had to be gone before the driver came out of his tent. I had to be gone before Carlick opened the cabin door.

The rope began to fray. Frantically, I chewed harder. With one last chomp, I broke it in two. I leaped to my feet, energy coursing through me. *Free!*

I sniffed Blue, then Cody. Snow covered them both like blankets. My sled mates didn't move in their warm cocoons. When they awoke, I would be gone.

Without a backward glance, I set off for the streets of Nome.

CHAPTER TWO

Nome

June 6, 1900

The sun peeked over the horizon as I trotted down the snow-packed street. A few flakes swirled from the graying sky, but the storm had ended. Wood buildings flanked each side of the narrow way, leaning in the wind. Shutters banged. Ahead of me, music and friendly sounds came from one of the lighted buildings.

A group of men stood on the stoop. I approached them with a wag of my tail.

"Get outta here, skinny cur!" One of the men threw a snowball at me.

"There should be a law that says any stray lurking on Front Street can be shot," another said, flicking his cigarette at my feet.

"Law?" a third asked with a chuckle. "What's that?"

I slunk into the shadows, where a pack of dogs tussled over food. My insides rumbled emptily. One of them growled at me, and I flattened my ears and looked at the ground. When they saw I was not a threat, they kept eating. But I knew from their bristled hair that I wasn't welcome.

I smelled salty water. Water meant fish. I trotted from the street to a stretch of frozen sand by the sea. As the sun rose higher, it glistened off piles of snow. I gazed toward the horizon, listening to the crash and boom of the ice breaking apart.

Row after row of tents extended to the edge of the water. Sleepy-eyed men were slowly emerging from some of them. My ears pricked. Were they friendly? Or would they treat me the way Carlick had?

Tired now, I walked among them, hoping for a

whistle or an encouraging "Here, boy. Have a bite of breakfast." But few glanced my way, and those who did had hard, uninviting eyes.

My stomach rumbled. Lowering my nose to the sand, I trotted along the edge of the water, hunting for washed-up fish. I smelled decay and rot and found a pile of bones and slimy scales. Then the rich scent of boiling walrus reached me.

Under the wood pilings of a dock, an Inupiaq family camped. They wore fur hoods against the morning cold. One had a baby strapped to her front. She stirred an iron pot over a driftwood fire. All three watched me, only their dark eyes moving.

Then the largest one held out a sliver of meat. *Food!* I stepped toward him, but glanced up at his face. There was no smile, and I spotted a leather strap in his other hand.

I leaped away. He raced after me. I galloped along the shoreline and then darted between stacks of wood crates that reached to the sky. I hid in the dark crevice and waited.

When I peered out, the man was still there. Again, he held out the meat for me but the leather strap lay at his feet.

I retreated into my hiding place. There was no other way out of the tunnel under the boxes. I was trapped.

Exhausted, I lay my head on my front legs. Night would fall. I would wait.

My belly ached. Many days had passed since I had arrived in Nome with little food. Dark nights prowling for a meal and sunlit days hiding in the tunnel had left me weak.

I needed to eat.

I trotted through the sea of tents to the shoreline. Two men worked on the beach. Their attention was on the sand that they shoveled and sifted. If they had seen me, they would have chased me away. A dog as a pet would mean less food for them. Or they might try and catch me since the quick sale of a dog to a driver might bring in needed money. To a hungry native, a dog might also mean a meal in a stew pot.

A dying fish flopped in the sand. Licking my lips, I pounced on it.

A boot found my ribs before my claws found the fish. "Get, before I kick you clean to Seattle!" I skittered away.

More men rose from their tents to start their day. I hid behind a barrel and watched for a dropped morsel or untended pot.

Two men stirred the coals of a smoky fire.

"Gotta get to work," one said to the other. "I heard a ship's arriving soon. More men coming with high hopes of finding gold."

The second man grunted. "That means more men with big dreams coming to steal our claim."

I heard a sizzle and sniffed the air. *Bacon.* Once before I had risked a hot pan and burning coals for bacon—and I had almost gotten shot.

I dared not risk it again.

I sneaked away, darting between tents, wooden pilings, and crates, still looking for something to eat. My eyes widened. Someone had left an open can sitting on a rock. Sprinting forward, I grabbed it in my powerful jaws and raced to my hiding place.

Beans. I lapped them from the can, careful of the sharp edge, and from the ground where some of them had spilled. Not as good as bacon, but at least they filled my belly. Now I could fall asleep for a bit.

Daytime was dangerous. I would come out again when night fell. In Nome, that was a long time from now. The sun seemed to sit in the sky forever.

Closing my eyes, I dreamed of a home filled with kind words—and maybe even bacon.

Night. There was no moon, no stars, but Front Street was lighted by torches and lanterns. Music and laughter rang from buildings brimming with people. Men strode down the wooden walkways and staggered into the muddy streets. I stuck to the lighted byways, searching for food left in trash cans or bones tossed from a doorway.

A man lay sprawled on his back in an alley. Though he seemed to be no threat, I gave him a wide berth.

My nose picked up the scent of bread. A half-eaten loaf, soggy and dirty, poked from a snowdrift by the front steps of a building. Men lingered on the top of the steps, smoking. Did I dare?

My aching belly gave me no choice.

Rushing from the shadows, I snatched the bread and ran under the wooden steps. It was gone in two bites. Voices rose above me.

"Hey, Carlick, was that the beast of a dog you've been looking for?"

Carlick. Even after all this time, I knew that name.

"Might be. If you can catch him, I'll pay a reward."

"How much?"

"Ten dollars."

"Sounds like easy money to me."

I heard the clomp of boots, and then a face peered at me. My heart beat faster.

"Hungry, boy?" The man sounded friendly. He held out a sausage link.

I drooled. I was so hungry.

"I've been trying to catch that blasted dog for three weeks," Carlick said. "Name's Murphy. There's a brand on his shoulder. If you gents can snag him, I'll throw in a round of whiskey."

A flurry of boots thundered above and around me. "Hurry and get behind him on the other side of the steps!" A hand grabbed my tail.

Panicking, I barreled forward and leaped from under the steps, knocking one of them clean off his feet.

"Hey!"

I didn't dare look over my shoulder, but I could tell by the pounding of feet that more than one person was after me.

"Get that dog! Fifteen-dollar reward!"

I ducked under a parked wagon and burst out the

other side. More men leaped off the wooden walk-way to my left and ran after me. I headed left, into a throng of people.

"Don't let him get away!"

I was surrounded. The only way out was to knock someone over. I was about to jump when I heard the crack of a whip.

"Let me at him!" Carlick said.

I sank to my belly.

Pushing through the men, Carlick approached me. "Finally I've got you. Now I'm going to teach you not to run away from me ever again." He raised the whip.

Whoo whoo! A ship's whistle blasted far in the dis-tance.

"It's the *Tacoma*!" someone shouted. "Thank the Lord she's finally here. Fresh supplies!"

In a wave, the men scurried toward the beach like rats. Carlick hollered after them to stop, but none turned around. Suddenly he was alone.

I lifted my lip in a snarl. Once I might have been

able to take him. I used to be as big and strong as a man. But now I was thin and weak—and frightened of that whip. I had known the sting of it too many times. Tucking my tail, I fled into the dark.

"I'll get you yet, you miserable cur!" Carlick shouted. "And then you'll wish you were *dead*."

I had escaped again. I knew next time I might not be so lucky.

CHAPTER THREE

A Friend

June 23, 1900

A crowd lined the beach, but the men were so intent on the ship anchored out in the sea that no one noticed me. I hid under a freight wagon and watched barges heading out to the *Tacoma*. Chunks of ice floated in the waves and clunked against the pilings. Worn out, I lay on the cold sand and propped my head on my paws.

Carlick was already there, standing on the other side of the wagon. I heard his voice before I saw him.

"Sure, the *Tacoma* is bringing fresh food," he told

several men clustered around him. "After the hard week, we need supplies. But it's going to bring more gold hunters, wanting to file claims."

"You and McKenzie have claimed land already," one of the men said.

"True—but we want more. We're looking at claiming farther up the Snake River and putting it in the name of Alaska Gold Mining Company too." Carlick handed one of the men some papers. "This has been approved by Judge Noyes. Get it done as soon as the courthouse opens. McKenzie and I don't want that river land in some stampeder's name. Let the newcomers mine the beach."

"Yes, sir." The man hurried off with the papers.

The barges began to return to shore. This time they overflowed with people. My ears tipped forward. Would one of the arrivals be friendly? Would someone offer me a home? The thought made me brave. As the first boats grew closer, I ventured from under the wagon.

The barges stopped offshore, and men in waist-high boots sloshed through the waves carrying people, boxes, and bags to the beach. Chattering and yelling filled the air.

I slunk closer, trying to see the faces of the new-comers. I saw exhaustion, misery, and disbelief. Their words sounded gruff.

"*This* is Nome?"

"Lord, it's the *end* of the earth."

"Don't drop that valise, man; it's my life savings."

"We need to take the first ship that's bound for Seattle."

"Not on the *Tacoma*. Never again."

Others nattered on and on about *gold,* just like Carlick.

"Gold on the beaches."

"Gold in the sand."

"Enough to make us rich!"

"We'll go back to the States with bulging pockets."

Barge after barge dropped off people and cargo and the crowd grew larger, but my hopes began to fade. No one seemed to have a kind word for a dog. Then I heard it: excited chattering like a noisy gull arriving for spring.

"Mama, we're here! This must be the pot at the end of the rainbow, just like in my books!"

I peered toward the water. A woman and a girl were riding on the shoulders of two burly men, who carried them through the surf to the beach.

"But where is the golden sand?" the girl asked. "And the ten-foot-high snowdrifts? Where are the moose and grizzly bears? And the ptarmigan and the tundra? Oh, I want to explore it all!"

"Be still, Sally. Or you will fall into the sea."

I raised my eyes to their faces. The girl's was flushed with joy, the woman's pale with a hint of hope. Longing filled me. Might these two be my new family?

The men set them on the beach, and others delivered a trunk, a crate, and several large bags. Only then did the woman's expression grow uncertain.

"I got my sea legs on the *Tacoma*," the girl said

as she wobbled to and fro. "Now I need to get my Nome legs."

"Stay close, Sally." The woman glanced uneasily around her. "We must find someone to help carry our belongings."

"We don't need help." Sally grabbed the end of the trunk and began to drag it up across the sand, away from the water and closer toward me. "We will prove to Grandmama and all the naysayers of San Francisco that we can survive in Nome."

Mama gave a huge sigh. "That may be harder than I thought."

"Grandpapa taught us to pitch a tent," Sally said. "And how to build and start a fire. It's good he's made many trips to Alaska and could show us how to bone a fish and skin a hare." She dropped her load in the sand.

"Careful with that trunk, darling." Mama picked up a bag in each hand. "My typewriter is packed in there. It will be our livelihood."

Most of the crowd had moved away, headed

toward the barges filled with supplies. Sally sat on top of the trunk and dabbed at her face with her pinafore.

This was my chance.

I crawled from behind the barrel, wagging my tail. Once it had been full and silky. Now it was dirty and thin. As I crept toward her, I lifted my lip in a grin, hoping she would see the dog I used to be.

Sally's mouth dropped open and her eyes filled with wonder. She dropped to her knees and wrapped her arms around me. "Oh! You are the most hand-some animal I have ever seen!"

"Sally!" Mama's voice was harsh, and I cringed. "What are you doing? That creature is huge, and look, he is snarling! Get away from him before he bites you."

"He is *not* snarling," Sally scoffed. "That is a smile. He is welcoming us to Nome."

"He is dirty. He must be a stray."

"No. He has a name." Her fingers found my collar. "Look, his brass tag says Murphy."

"Then he has a home to go to. Leave him be. We have enough to worry about. We must find a hotel to stay in before night falls."

"It won't be dark until midnight." Sally ran her fingers gently down my spine. "And he does not have a home. He's skin and bones, and there are scars under his fur. He needs a washing and brushing and a good meal."

"You and I need a washing and brushing and a good meal." Mama pushed a stray hair under her hat.

Two men approached. Their smiles were pleasant, but I felt the threat of danger that hung around them. There were few women in Nome and even fewer girls. What did these men want with Mama and Sally? My hackles rose.

"Ma'am." One tipped a dirty hat. "We'll help you with your luggage."

"Thank you, but no," Mama's voice was gracious, but she sounded anxious.

The larger one stepped closer. "I wasn't asking for your permission."

Sally grabbed my collar. "And she wasn't asking for your assistance. Now leave us be or I will command my dog to attack."

I growled, hoping to sound brave. Could they sense I was not?

The men glanced at me, then at Sally. For someone so little, her courage was so big.

"Next time, perhaps, ma'am," one said. They disappeared into the throng of people and freight.

Sally blew out her breath. "See? Murphy has already proved that he's our protector." She enveloped me in another hug. "Nome may be our salvation, but it will also be dangerous. We need him, Mama, as much as he needs us."

"I think you're right, my brave but foolish daughter. Thank you for welcoming us to Nome, Murphy." Mama patted me then and I could feel the exhaustion in her touch. "We have meager supplies and no firm plans for where to stay for the night, but if you would like, you are invited to join our small family."

Family. I gave Sally a slobbery kiss, then nuzzled Mama's hand. Stooping, she gave me a hard hug and I saw tears glimmering in her eyes.

CHAPTER FOUR

Beaches of Gold

June 28, 1900

This rope goes here." Sally hammered a wooden stake into the sand.

The tent was halfway up, and it flapped in the chilly wind. I tried to help by holding the stakes in my mouth until she and Mama needed them.

Sally and Mama had stayed at a boarding house run by a family called Owen for many days while they found their bearings in Nome and the right place to pitch their tent. No dogs were allowed inside the boarding house, so I slept in the livery with two skinny horses. Sally visited me every day, but the

barn was not a home. I was excited when they chose a spot on the beach and moved out of the boarding house.

Crouching, Sally studied the ground. "Look Mama, there *is* gold in the sand, just like Mr. Owens said." Letting some slip through her fingers, she picked out several small flakes.

"We're not here for the gold," Mama said. "We'll make a living off the prospectors and shopkeepers. They will need advertising, contracts, and wills."

Poking her head around the side of the tent, she added, "And letters home."

"But if we find gold, you won't have to work in an office." Sally dug again in the sand. "We can stake our own claim and find enough nuggets to buy a house for the winter."

"That is *if* we stay." Mama bent over to pound a stake. "You've heard your grandfather's stories about Nome winters."

I barked for them to hurry. Summer nights were cold in Alaska; we needed to finish getting the tent up. When the sun finally fell, so would the temperature. Sudden storms sometimes blew in from the sea without warning, and shelter was important. Prickles of fear filled me as the sun dropped lower in the sky—and not just because of the weather.

Nome was a reckless town. Two ladies on the beach attracted a lot of attention, and many men had come by to introduce themselves this afternoon. All had been gentlemen, but that would not always be true. Darkness brought out the worst in men. I needed to stay vigilant. And the tent needed to be up for some protection. I woofed again.

"Yes, we will hurry, Murphy." Sally checked the tent peg and rope. "We will all need a bath before turning in for the night. You smell like rotten fish and horse droppings, and I smell like cigar smoke and sauerkraut."

"I doubt the ladies of San Francisco would invite us to tea," Mama murmured.

Sally laughed. I jumped up to lick her cheek, my paws leaving black streaks on her pinafore. "Oh, Murphy, the ladies would definitely not invite us now," she said as she tried to brush off the dirt.

When the last stake was in and the tent secure, Sally, Mama, and I eyed it with pride.

"This is our new home," Sally said softly.

Home. The word sounded wonderful. As wonderful as *bacon.*

"For now," Mama said. "Let's hope we can save

enough for a cabin. Though with a can of peaches costing five dollars, we may spend all our money on food. Come. Let's gather fresh clothes and find a bathhouse. Mrs. Owens said the best one for ladies was in the Dexter Hotel."

Sally grabbed the end of the trunk and began to drag it inside the tent. When I tried to follow her, she shooed me away. "After your bath, Murphy."

There was that word again, *bath*. I had never heard it before.

"When you are clean, you can come in and help us organize our new home." She dropped the canvas flap.

I stared forlornly at the closed flap, my ears pricked so I could catch their voices. I didn't want to be away from them for an instant.

"Our money needs to be safe, Mama," Sally said. "We must have it with us at all times."

"It has stayed safe in the pocket I sewed in my bloomers."

"I should carry some as well. In case you are robbed."

"No gentleman would attempt to tear my bloomers!" Mama gasped.

"These are not all gentlemen."

Mama sighed. "You are correct, Sally. We were warned—there are no laws in Nome."

"Yes. Grandmama warned us of that at least ten times a day." Sally giggled.

"Perhaps we should have heeded her advice."

"Which has been as constant as the rising sun and as stern as a preacher's sermons—for the past twelve years of my life."

"You are only eleven, child."

"I know." They both broke into laughter. I did not know what made them so giddy, but the sound made me bark.

Sally threw open the flap. "Murphy says he is ready for his bath."

"I do not believe the hotel will allow a dog in its

washtub." Mama followed Sally out of the tent, carrying a satchel. "Especially not one as huge and filthy as Murphy."

"Then we will ask someone where the workers bathe. It will save us money as well."

Mama stopped. "Oh, Sally, are we lowering ourselves to the status of scullery maids already?"

"We must be practical, Mama, if we are to thrive in Nome—and escape Grandmama's grip." She shuddered, and I pressed my nose into her palm. She stroked my head. "Perhaps we will make our fortune with your typewriter. Perhaps we *will* find gold. I don't care how we survive, but we will. Because I will never go back to San Francisco and Grandmama's house. *Never.*"

I did not understand Sally's words. But I heard the determination in her voice. That same determination had helped me escape from Carlick. Tipping back my head, I bayed like a hound to let Sally know that I understood.

CHAPTER FIVE

Another Narrow Escape

June 28, 1900

Nome's beaches may be paved with gold, but Front Street is certainly not," Mama observed.

The three of us made our way down the wooden walkway. I strutted in between Sally and Mama, my fur fluffy and shiny, my spots glowing white. Now I knew what a bath was—it meant warm water and sweet soap. Sally and Mama were fresh and clean too.

Sally had taken off my collar, which had grown so small it dug into my neck. I was glad when she didn't put it back on. Instead she tucked it into Mama's satchel and tied a red scarf around my neck.

"I would say Front Street is paved in rascals," Sally said. She held a parasol open to block the light snow that drifted from the darkening sky. "I have counted four drunks, three pickpockets, and two hucksters, and the sun has not yet set."

Mama arched one brow. "And how do you know what a huckster looks like, young lady?"

"Grandpapa taught me to watch out for bears, moose, and hucksters." Sally gave Mama a sly look. "There were many in the Klondike when he was there. I have also counted at least fifty interested suitors and heard a hundred whistles. You are the prettiest lady in Nome."

"I appear to be the only *lady* in Nome," Mama said. "At least at this time of night."

"Murphy will have to be our guardian in this 'godforsaken town,' as Grandmama called it." Sally dug her fingers into the ruff of fur around my neck. I strutted, trying to look worthy.

"Nome does have some respectable stores among

the saloons and dance halls," Mama observed, stopping in front of the bakery. My nose twitched happily.

Sally gasped. "Fresh-baked bread! Can you work here, Mama?"

"Perhaps." Tipping her head back, she read the sign. "California Bakery... We must make note of all the shops and businesses where I can apply for employment. The bakery or the lumberyard might need inventory and accounts typed. Mrs. Owens suggested that Fox & Gibson might need claims and deeds recorded."

"Look! There's a circulating library!" Sally hurried up the walkway. The building was closed for the night, but she pressed her nose against the glass. "Perhaps they might let me borrow books in return for shelving them."

"Hey, lady!" Someone grabbed Mama's shoulder and rudely spun her around. "Where'd you get that dog?" A bearded man wearing a tattered bowler hat pointed at me.

I scooted away from him and hid behind Sally.

"Pardon me!" Mama yanked her arm from the man's grasp. "Do I know you, sir, for you to act so familiar?"

"No, ma'am. But I think I know that dog. He belongs to Carlick."

I recognized the man by his voice—and his smell. He'd held out the sausage link to me, trying to catch me for Carlick.

"There's a reward of fifteen dollars, and I aim to claim it." The man lunged for me, but I ducked farther behind Sally. Mama may have been speechless, but Sally was not.

"Get your hands off my dog!" she snapped, swatting him with her parasol.

With a yelp, he drew back. "That is *not* your dog," he sputtered. "Belongs to Carlick."

"What proof do you have?" Sally demanded, the parasol still raised like a club.

"Proof?" The man suddenly looked unsure of

himself. "Look, my name's Beckett. I don't mean no harm, but I believe that dog is Carlick's. We tried to catch him a while ago but he got away."

"That's not proof," Sally scoffed. "What is his name? What breed?"

"Uhhhh…" Beckett's face turned red under the barrage of questions. He shifted his eyes to the crowd that was forming around us. I stayed low behind Sally's skirts.

"Do you and your daughter need help, ma'am?" a man in a dapper suit asked.

"Thank you, sir," Mama murmured. "I believe my daughter and I can handle this unfortunate incident."

My heart hammered. Would Carlick's people take me away from my new family?

But most of the men seemed to only have eyes for Mama, who drew herself upright. "Mr. Beckett, does Carlick's dog have identification?" she asked.

"Well…um…" He shuffled his feet uneasily.

"Carlick's dog is big like this one, and Carlick said his dog has a collar with the name Murphy on it."

Sally didn't hesitate. "Our dog wears a silk scarf, not a collar."

Flushing, the man began to back away. "Yes, ma'am. I do see this dog has spots, and Carlick's dog is brown, so I apologize." Tipping his greasy hat, he quickly retreated. A few chuckles rang out from the group, and several people clapped.

Mama nodded our thanks and then took Sally's hand. "Grab Murphy," she whispered, and together we rushed down the walkway toward the beach.

When we were safely away from Front Street, Sally let go of my scarf and Mama let go of Sally's hand. "I am embarrassed that we had to resort to such dishonesty," she declared. "And oh, such disrespectful behavior from you, young lady."

"Grandmama would surely have whipped me for my words," Sally admitted. "But Mr. Beckett was no gentleman."

Mama lowered her voice. "We shall speak of Mr.

Beckett's accusation once we get in the tent."

We hurried across the sand, weaving around campfires, prospectors, and supplies.

Only when we were inside our own tent with the flap firmly tied shut did Mama blow out a relieved breath. She dropped her satchel and lighted a lantern.

Sally plopped down on her cot and pulled me close against her knee. Panting, I glanced around, liking the cozy area. A flowered rug was on the floor. Circling, I laid down on it, wondering if Sally and Mama would let me stay, now that I was clean.

"So, according to Mr. Beckett we are in possession of a dog that belongs to someone named Carlick," Mama said as she removed her coat.

Carlick. I could not escape that name.

"No," Sally said stubbornly. "Carlick's dog wears a collar."

Mama pulled the collar from her satchel and held it up. "You mean like this one?"

Sally refused to look at it. "And the man said

Carlick's dog wasn't spotted."

"You mean Carlick's dog was dirty brown, the color of Murphy before he was bathed?"

Sally flushed, but her eyes stayed stubborn. "Murphy belongs with us. If he loved this Carlick person, he would not have been living like a stray on the beach, all skinny and scarred."

"I agree. All God's creatures should be treated with dignity." Mama dropped the collar in Sally's lap. "But what are we to do about Carlick? He has even offered a reward."

"We'll just have to keep Murphy in the tent night and day," Sally said. "Until the men get tired of looking for him."

"That's not a realistic plan," Mama said. "Murphy would not like being penned up, and we need him to be your guardian while I work."

"It appears that he needs us to be *his* guardian as well." Sally held tightly to the scarf around my neck.

"I've got an idea." Smiling slyly, Mama lifted the lid of her trunk. Reaching inside, she pulled out a strange machine and set it on a small folding stool.

Sally's eyes widened. "What are you going to type, Mama?"

"Murphy needs a San Francisco dog license, I believe, with the name Sally Ann Dawson as owner. As well as a ticket of passage that states he boarded the *Tacoma* bound for Nome on June 1, 1900, in the company of his owner."

Squealing with joy, Sally jumped up and flung her arms around her mother. "Oh, Mama, I think you are the greatest huckster in all of Nome!" Picking up the collar, she added, "Murphy and I have a job to do too. Come, boy."

She untied the tent flap, and together we raced down to the water's edge. There, she flung the collar as far out to sea as she could. Then she held my head in both hands and looked me in the eye.

"You are no longer Carlick's dog," she said solemnly. "You are still Murphy, but now you belong to us."

For a second, the collar floated on top of the surf,

and then it disappeared. Pulling away from Sally, I bounded into the waves. I did not completely understand what had happened, but somehow I knew that I was free of Carlick, and it made me bark with joy.

CHAPTER SIX

Prospecting

August 3, 1900

Murphy, listen to the letter I wrote to Grand-papa," Sally said.

We sat on a rock that jutted into the rushing sea. Sally's bonnet flapped in the wind. A picnic of beef and dried apples was in an open basket on the sand by her feet.

I glanced at Sally when she spoke, but then my gaze returned to the Nome beach. I needed to watch for strange men, as well as for seagulls that might dare to steal our breakfast.

Dear Grandpapa and Grandmama,

Mama and I have a lovely seaside home with ocean views. We also have a strong friend named Murphy who is keeping us safe. He and I explore Nome every day. We talk to the miners—those who are successful as well as those who have gone bust. They all say that black sand is where you can find gold. I am learning all about mining so one day I can file my own claim.

Sally looked up from her letter. "Are you listening, Murphy? Or watching seagulls?"

I gave her a slurpy kiss.

"I need your advice. Should I add news about the swarms of mosquitoes and the thieving ne'er-do-wells? Grandpapa would be interested. But I worry that Grandmama will send an army to retrieve us."

Jumping off the rock, I barked at a gull that flew too close to our picnic basket.

"Perhaps you are right. I won't mention the mosquitoes or the five murders on Front Street." She picked up the letter again.

Even though it is 93 degrees during the day, there are still icebergs on the Bering Sea because it freezes at night when the sun goes down.

Mama makes $1.25 per hour typing and filing claims at Fox & Gibson Surveyors. In the evening, miners dictate their letters to her. They are all homesick. I take the letters to the post office the next day and then I deliver mail for Mr. O'Malley, the postal clerk.

"I won't mention that Mama works day and night and falls into bed exhausted," she told me. "And that I earn extra money delivering mail to saloons and dance halls. Even Grandpapa might object."

A second seagull swooped low, aiming for the open tin of beef. I snapped at its gray tail feathers, and it flew off with a raucous squawk.

48

"Thank you for saving our breakfast, Murphy." Sally threw me the last chunk of beef and I gulped it quickly.

"Now settle down and let me finish reading you this letter," she scolded. "You are mentioned again, so be patient."

I have met a friend named See-ya-yuk. He is Inu-piaq. One day we were fishing in the same spot. He smiled a shy hello. Since then he has showed me how to catch mackerel and codfish. You would be jealous of all the fish we catch, Grandpapa.

Please send apples from our trees back home and chocolate and jam with your next package. Murphy loves sweets.

Love and kisses,
Sally

"See? I told you that you were mentioned again. I should have said 'send a ham hock since Murphy eats more than a horse.' Mama admits you are worth it though, for her peace of mind." Sally ruffled my ears. "Speaking of Mama, we'd best get back before she leaves." She packed up the basket, and we made our way past other miners, rotten timber, abandoned equipment, and piles of sand.

When we reached the tent, Mama bustled out, her brow knit. She wore her shawl and brimmed day hat. "There you are, Sally. Don't forget to come by the assayer's office. Mr. Fox has papers for you to file."

"Yes, ma'am."

"And we need wood for the fire, and we are out of tinned beef. Oh, the chores are never-ending." Her frown deepened when she saw the picnic basket. "Have you been feeding Murphy from our meager food supplies?"

"Ummm…" Sally looked at her feet, and I snuffled a rock on the ground.

Mama sighed. "No wonder we are out of beef. Now hurry and clean up. I will see you later at the office."

"Yes, ma'am."

Sally watched her mother weave around the tents until she disappeared. "I worry about her, Murphy. Nome was to be a grand adventure, except Mama has grown too tired to enjoy it."

After securing the tent, Sally and I headed toward Front Street, walking along the shoreline. She spied a rusty miner's pan half buried in the sand.

"This is just what we'll need when we have our own claim." Pulling it out, she brushed it off. "I'll add it to our stash of supplies. Soon, we will be able to strike out on our own."

She chattered away as we continued walking. "I have saved almost enough money to file a claim. Grandpapa says Alaska's winter weather shows its ugly head in September. It's already the first of August, so we don't have much time. Oh, look, there's Mr. Smithson." She waved at a man who stood knee-deep in water, shoveling sand into a sluice box. "Perhaps we can get a panning lesson from him."

Sally set the pan on the shore and waded into the water, the surf lapping the ankles of her gum boots.

"Hello, Mr. Smithson." I followed her, the frigid water tickling my belly.

Sally inspected the bottom of the slanted wooden chute for sparkly flakes of gold. I stood next to Mr. Smithson. Sometimes he shoveled up fish and I got to eat them.

"Any luck today?" she asked him.

"Naw." Mr. Smithson wiped his forehead, which glistened under his droopy hat. The sun was heating up. "Gold's about gone from the beach sand. Too

many fools out here prospecting. We need another meteor shower."

Sally giggled. "The gold does not come from outer space, Mr. Smithson."

He crooked one brow. "So you believe crazy Leibowitz's theory that it rose from the earth in a volcano?"

"No. I believe it washes down from the rivers and creeks. That's what Mr. Fox says, so I'm staking my claim on the Snake River."

"That's loonier than a meteor shower." Mr. Smithson snorted. "If it was true, then the men who have claims inland would be rich."

Sally stared wistfully toward the tundra. "Some of them are getting rich. Especially those who are mining Anvil and Dexter Creeks. And if Mama and I are to stay in Alaska, we need to find enough gold to buy a cabin."

Mr. Smithson continued shoveling. "The only ones getting rich are the companies that are jumping claims that already yield gold, like McKenzie and Carlick. Their company is mining most of the land on the Snake, so you'll have a tough time getting a spot."

I swung my head up at the mention of Carlick's name. Sally slid a protective arm around my neck. "I thought their company only held claims along the creeks."

"Not anymore. Those two have Judge Noyes in their pockets. They've been staking claims along the Snake, too, only the claims already belong to other men. Carlick and McKenzie pay off Judge Noyes, who stonewalls the real owners while he and his gang set up mining operations."

"That doesn't sound right!" Sally's voice rose.

"It ain't. Those two remind me of Mr. George and his son, who owned me, my family, and the land where we picked cotton. Men like them think they rule the world and they can do whatever they want. And McKenzie and Carlick, why, they practically rule Nome."

"Like kings?" Sally asked.

"Like masters." He dropped his shovel and poured buckets of water onto the chute. The water carried the sand back down to the sea and any gold that was heavier than the sand fell to the bottom of the chute and got trapped in the riffles.

"Can no one stop them?" Sally asked as she again leaned over the chute.

Mr. Smithson shrugged. "So far, no."

"Oh!" Sally held up a nugget the size of a nail

head. "Mr. Smithson, I believe it will buy you food for a week."

"Young lady, you are a godsend. Perhaps there *was* a meteor shower last night." He winked. "Here's a little 'flour' for your help," he added, giving Sally a pinch of gold dust from the sluice.

"Thank you, Mr. Smithson." Carefully she sprinkled it into a silver vial that hung from a leather strap around her neck. "Tell me, if you were mining on the Snake, what equipment would you take?"

"A good pan like this one you set on the sand." Mr. Smithson said. He picked it up, scooped sand and water into it, and then rocked it back and forth. "See how it separates out the gold?"

"Let me try."

I hunted for fish in the surf while Sally concentrated on her pan. Gold held no interest for me.

Finally she stood. "I must get to the post office," she told Mr. Smithson. "Thank you for showing me how to pan."

"Come back after you finish your mail delivering, Miss Sally. You and your dog are my good luck charms."

"We'll return," Sally said. "I need another lesson on finding gold. But now we need to hurry before Mr. O'Malley has a fit."

We slogged up the muddy path toward Front Street. "I do believe we need to find out more about Carlick," she told me. "If he is as disagreeable as Mr. Smithson says, no wonder you ran away from him."

We had not encountered Carlick as we roamed the streets of Nome over the past weeks. Today was the first time I had heard his name in a long while. This was fine with me. Even if I did see him again, I didn't know if he would recognize me. I was now lean and fit with a glossy coat. As I trotted down the walkway by Sally's side, I had a spring in my step and a gleam in my eye.

Still, sometimes I thought I saw him. At times, I thought I heard his voice. And when I did, I remembered the sting of his whip and I cowered.

CHAPTER SEVEN

Miss Sally's Dog

August 3, 1900

Accompanying Sally on her journeys around Nome was my favorite part of the day. Since she picked up and delivered mail, she knew everyone. She collected pennies as payment, and I was petted and fed scraps. No longer did the shopkeepers see me as a stray. Now I was Miss Sally's dog.

A long line of people stood in front of the post office, waiting to post or pick up mail. Sally skirted around the men and ducked into the small building. She handed Mr. O'Malley the letters Mama had typed last night. "Each is sealed, addressed, and has

a two-cent stamp, sir," she told him.

"Thank you, Miss Sally. I have another stack to fill your bag. Remind everyone that the steamship *Lucky Lady* will be arriving in about four days and then departing the next day for Seattle. The mail to the mainland will go with it."

"I will, sir." Sally grabbed the bulging satchel, and we walked to the Dexter Hotel.

"Good day, Mr. Wyatt Earp." Sally shook hands with a slightly rotund, very tall man who stood outside.

"Good day, Miss Sally." He patted my head. "And good day to your dog. Any mail for me?"

She handed him three envelopes, and he gave her several coins. "A serious question, Mr. Earp. If you were mining along the Snake River, what equipment would you take?"

"A warm quilt and a deck of faro cards," he replied, a twinkle in his eye.

"I'll remember the quilt. Thank you, sir." She bid him farewell, and we left the Dexter Hotel.

A ragtag group of boys strolling down the muddy street stopped to toss stones at me. I yelped and darted under a wagon bed. "Look at the big coward run!" one shouted. "What a scaredy-cat!"

Sally glared at him. "You're the scaredy-cat, Johnny Tucker! Otherwise you wouldn't hang back and throw stones. You'd come right over so I could sock you in the nose."

Putting his fists on his hips, Johnny shot Sally a smug look. "I jest might."

Just then Mr. Earp stepped out onto the street to survey the situation, and the boys left, grumbling. I crawled from under the wagon, tail tucked. I wished I had barked and frightened them off myself, but once again I had run.

"Ignore their meanness, Murphy," Mr. Earp said as he gave me a pat. "I have learned that a showdown is a last resort."

Sally and I continued on our way to the Horse-shoe Saloon. "Good morning, Miss Althea," Sally said as we entered the main room, which was dark even though it was midday. A woman with rouged cheeks sat at a round wooden table, eating breakfast. She—and her bacon—smelled delicious.

"Good morning, Sally, and good morning to you, you handsome boy." Cupping my head, she kissed me over and over until I squirmed.

Sally handed her several letters. Miss Althea gave her some coins and fed me a strip of bacon.

"Miss Althea, if you were mining on the Snake, what equipment would you take?" Sally asked.

Miss Althea chewed a bite of egg. The she dabbed her lips with a linen napkin and said, "I would take mosquito netting and a bottle of whiskey."

"I will surely add the netting to my list," Sally said. Waving goodbye, she led me back into the daylight.

"The money is adding up, Murphy." Sally patted her pocket. "Soon we will be ready to file a claim."

Our next stop was a house on the edge of town. The Hughes brothers sat in front of their cabin, smoking their pipes and cleaning their rifles. The two brothers looked just alike, with shaggy beards and long hair, which they said kept away the mosquitoes. The only difference between them was that one brother spoke; the other just grunted. "Good day, Miss Sally," the talkative brother said.

"Hello, Mr. Hughes," Sally said. "I have some mail for you."

"Thank you, Miss Sally." He took the stack. "My brother and I won't need you to deliver our mail much longer. We've decided to leave Nome."

"But why, sir?" Sally asked.

"Winter in Nome is close to purgatory. Do you know anyone who might be interested in purchasing our cabin?"

Sally's eyes brightened. "Oh, yes! Mama and I need a new abode before winter comes. How much will your fine cabin cost?"

"To you and your lovely mother I would sell it for twenty dollars. We'll be leaving in September."

"I will tell Mama," she said. "Thank you, sirs." Sally waved goodbye, and we left.

"Mama will be so excited!" Sally exclaimed as we

trotted back to town. I could feel her joy in the drum of her boots on the wooden walkway.

A cat darted from a doorway. I gave chase, but when it turned and hissed, I stopped in my tracks and it skittered off. I told myself the cats were necessary to catch the rats—and that I was not afraid.

When we reached Fox & Gibson, Sally burst through the door. "Mama! Wait until you hear my news!"

Mama was hunched over a ledger, writing. She didn't look up even when Sally started chattering like a gull.

"The Hughes brothers are selling their cabin for twenty dollars. They're leaving in September. It has a stove and a chimney and is made of sturdy logs. See-ya-yuk can show me how to chink between the logs and hang skins for warmth—"

"Hush, Sally," Mama cut in, her voice flat. She paused, her pen hovering over the ledger. Glancing over her shoulder, she caught the eye of Mr. Fox, who was frowning at us.

"Is there a problem, Mrs. Dawson?" he asked, his words clipped. I flattened myself on the floor behind the counter. Mr. Fox did not like me in the shop. "This is a respectable business, not a kennel," he had told Sally.

"No problem, Mr. Fox!" Mama sounded cheery now. Then she turned back to Sally. "I am busy and you have filing to do, young lady."

Sally's smile faded. "Yes, ma'am."

Mama stood and nodded toward the door. "Let's put Murphy outside."

"Yes, ma'am. Come on, Murphy." I followed Sally and Mama out to the front stoop, my head hanging.

"I heard what you said about the Hughes brothers' cabin," Mama said, lowering her voice. "But we have made no decision about staying the winter. Your grandfather has written that he is coming to Nome on business. We will discuss the matter with him when he arrives."

"I don't need to discuss the matter!" Sally cried out. "I *have* made a decision! I won't return to Grandmama's house and her harsh rules. Nome is my home now. Winter will be hard, but the Hughes cabin is ten steps from town."

Mama rubbed the bridge of her nose. Men passed by, tipping their hats, and she smiled politely. I wagged my tail, hoping to make her feel better, but it was as if she didn't see me.

"We need more than a cabin, Sally," she finally said. "We need wood and supplies to last from October when the sea freezes until April when it thaws."

"I have saved money" Sally reached into the pocket of her pinafore and pulled out her pennies. "And when I find gold, we will have enough—"

"Stop speaking of gold!" Taking Sally by the shoulders, Mama gave her a good shake. "Haven't you learned anything from the miners? Few strike it rich. I see those who have tried come in to Fox & Gibson, penniless and broken. They don't have enough coins for fare back to Seattle."

"But there are those who do find gold," Sally protested.

"The large companies that employ twenty men. You are a child, Sally. Wipe that foolish dream from your head and come in and do your work before Mr. Fox fires us both." Mama gave Sally another shake. Then, turning, she strode back into the office with a swish of her skirts.

For a moment, Sally was silent. Then she stroked my ears. "I'm sorry you had to hear that, Murphy. And I am sorry you have to stay out here, but I won't be long."

I whined, trying to tell Sally that it would be okay and that I was sad for her. Mama had never yelled before, and never had I seen her shake Sally.

"I'm sorry that Mama isn't excited about the cabin." Sighing, she leaned over and rested her head on top of mine. "But what I am *really* sorry about is that every day the Mama I love grows more and more like the Grandmama I hope never to see again."

CHAPTER EIGHT

Mukluks

August 5, 1900

 oday you will practice wearing your harness."
Sally slipped a canvas coat over my head and
buckled it around my stomach.

She had sewn fur on the buckles and on the straps
that hugged my neck to keep them from chafing.
Four leather ties hung from each side. She attached
a bucket to those on one side and a rope to those on
the other.

We were in front of the tent, readying for a day
on the tundra. The sun was already hot, and when I
shook my head, drool flew in the air.

"After we visit See-ya-yuk and go fishing, we'll collect wood that I'll tie to your harness. I'll see how strong you really are," Sally went on. "When we are on our own, panning for gold, you will need to haul the wood."

Since that day Mama had given Sally a shake, Sally often talked to me of "our claim" and "finding gold." I wasn't quite sure what she meant, but I did know one thing—she never talked again to Mama about this trip.

I took a step, and the bucket rattled. Slowly I had been getting used to this strange harness. I did not mind it as much as the pulling harness, and of course, I would do anything for Sally.

"See-ya-yuk's mother has finished my mukluks. I'll need them for cold nights on the tundra." Bending, she held my head in her hands and stared into my eyes. "Mama may *think* that gold has been knocked from my head. But she is wrong. And when we find that big nugget and buy the Hughes brothers' cabin, she will change her mind about staying." She kissed me on the top of my muzzle, and I gave her a wet kiss in return. Then, standing, she swung her satchel over her shoulder and we headed into town.

"What can I trade for the mukluks?" Sally mused aloud as we walked past the stores. "Our money does not mean much to the Inupiaq."

We passed the bakery. Lifting my nose, I sniffed deeply. Sally's eyes brightened. "Of course! See-ya-yuk and his family love freshly baked bread."

The bell over the door rang when we went into the bakery. "Hello, Mrs. McConnell." The tall woman behind the counter wore a white apron over her long skirts. She smelled as heavenly as Miss Althea at the saloon.

Sally purchased several loaves and tucked them in her satchel. "Mrs. McConnell, if you were mining gold on the Snake River, what would you take?"

"A bag of biscuits. They keep forever and are still delicious even if they get hard or wet. Plus your dog loves them." Plucking a biscuit from its stack, Mrs. McConnell tossed one to me. I snatched it from the air and gulped it down in one bite.

"I will keep biscuits in mind." We left the bakery and turned down an alley. Behind the rows of buildings on Front Street, the tundra stretched for miles like a green sea.

I led the way up the path that wound from town. The frozen earth had partially melted under the hot sun, and my paws squished into the mushy ground. Around us, the hills were colorful with wildflowers. Sally picked handfuls of phlox and wild geraniums, which grew among the tundra grass. I dug in the sweet-smelling violets, kicking dirt in the air.

"Oh look—the first blueberries of the season!" Sally said after we had walked about a mile. The squat bushes were scattered in a brushy area of willow. "We'll pick some on the way home for dinner tonight, Murphy. Though a handful now sure would taste wonderful."

Plopping beside Sally, I delicately plucked a clump from a twig.

She giggled as she filled her own mouth. "You are

like a bear, eating whatever you can find. Which is good. When we are on the claim on the Snake River, we will be living off the land."

See-ya-yuk's dogs let out a terrible racket as we approached the family's summer home, a tent made of skins. Small and wolflike, they charged toward us, hair bristling. My own hair rose, but I ducked behind Sally to get away from them.

She swatted at them with her satchel. "Go away, you foolish dogs," she scolded. "Or you will get no bread heels."

See-ya-yuk ran over, a grin filling his brown face. He wore mukluks, boy's breeches, a fur vest, and a wool military cap. "Sally! Your boots are ready. They are in the *ee-nih*."

Sally clapped her hands together. "Thank you! And I brought you a present too."

See-ya-yuk raced to Sally's side and yanked open her satchel. The natives were always curious and would even come uninvited into Sally and Mama's tent if I did not bar the door.

"Aye-ee!" See-ya-yuk pulled out a bread loaf.

Carrying the bread, he raced to his home, shouting for his mother. The dogs chased after him, forgetting about me, and I barked at their retreating tails.

Sally laughed. "Save your false bravado for bears and wolves," she told me.

See-ya-yuk's little brother toddled out from the triangle doorway and over to us. I licked Wee-lil-tuk's cheek; he always tasted like seal liver, my favorite. Squealing with laughter, he fell on his bottom.

Sally pulled off her bonnet and handed it to him. Wee-lil-tuk put it backwards on his head, which made her laugh.

See-ya-yuk popped his head around the tent flap and proudly held up the mukluks his mother had made. "For you, Sally."

"Oh!" she gasped. "They are beautiful! Please tell Nee-ok-see-na how much I like them."

The boots were made of walrus hide. The skin on the outside was pliable and waterproof, while the fur on the inside was soft and warm. Sally and I had watched See-ya-yuk's mother as she worked on them, shaping the skin with her teeth. Sally had practiced too, which is how she had learned how to make the straps for my harness. My own mouth had watered as they worked, until Nee-ok-see-na had laughingly thrown me a chunk of seal meat to chew.

"I'll never wear my stiff old boots again." Sally sat on the ground and pulled off her gum boots.

See-ya-yuk's eyes widened. "For me?" he asked, lifting the boot she had taken off.

"If you can fit into them." Sally handed him the second boot.

He attempted to fit one over his foot. "Small," he said solemnly. Whipping his knife from his belt, he split the end of the boot and shoved his foot inside. His toes wiggled. "Fits!"

See-ya-yuk put the other boot on and then rose and danced around. I woofed, the native dogs howled, and Wee-lil-tuk squealed as Sally danced in her knee-high mukluks.

Nee-ok-see-na emerged from the tent, bringing everyone—even me—bread slices slathered with fat. We ate heartily.

"Now *aqalugniaqtuq*—fishing," See-ya-yuk said, licking the fat off his fingers. Sally picked up her satchel and we headed down to the river. By the time we reached a quiet spot on the Snake, the sun was high in the sky.

"I'll surprise Mama with fish and blueberries for dinner." Sally threaded a sliver of tomcod onto the hook. She knew well how to bait the bone hook and cast out. But often she lost her trout or grayling before bringing it to shallow water. I tried to help, catching them in my mouth when I could. But fish are slippery and wiggly, and usually I lost them too.

I waited in front of her, my paws in the cold, swirling water, my eyes searching for a flash of silver or red.

See-ya-yuk was a patient and quiet fisherman like me, but Sally was as noisy as the native dogs who

crashed about on the shore yelping at hares. "See-ya-yuk!" she called. "I see gold in the water. Wouldn't it be better to fish for gold instead of trout? Then you could buy a two-bedroom cabin for your mother. Isn't that a nugget by that rock?"

See-ya-yuk nodded but kept his eyes on the bobbing chunk of wood tied to his line. As the sun sank lower, he pulled in fish after fish.

"This would not even feed Wee-lil-tuk." Sally stared at the one fish that she had caught. "I must get better at fishing if we are to survive on our own."

See-ya-yuk handed her a large trout that he had caught. "For Mrs. Dawson," he said with a grin.

"Mama will appreciate this. Thank you." Sally wrapped her two fish in oilcloth and tucked them in her satchel. She waved goodbye to See-ya-yuk, and we headed down the trail. The dogs followed us for a while, snapping playfully at my tail. I tucked it between my legs until they grew tired of the game and left.

As we walked, Sally picked up fallen branches and tied them to both sides of my harness. Soon I was loaded down with sticks while the bucket still clanked on one side.

When we reached the patch of blueberry bushes that grew on a sunny hillside, Sally untied the bucket. She picked berries, tossing them into the bucket as she sang a song, timing the words with each plink. I ate berries straight off the bushes.

Twigs snapped, startling me, and I spun around. A moose stood over me, its head lowered. I could tell by her flat ears and the raised hair on her hump that she was angry. I knew a female moose will not usually attack—unless she is protecting a calf.

Slowly I backed up, my gaze searching for a sign of her young. Moose have big flat hooves that can strike hard, and I did not want to get pummeled. Then I saw the calf, flicking its ears at the flies. It was on the other side of Sally, who was bent over intently searching for ripe berries. We had not seen it as we picked because it was half-hidden in the brush.

My heart began to pound. Sally was directly between the moose and her baby!

CHAPTER NINE
A Sudden Change

August 5, 1900

Grabbing Sally's long skirt in my teeth, I yanked her out of the path between the moose and her calf. The cloth tore and she fell. Her bucket tipped over and blueberries scattered everywhere.

"Murphy!" She swatted me on the nose.

Sally had never hit me before, and the pain startled me. For an instant, I remembered my days with Carlick and was filled with sadness, but then the moose stepped closer to us.

She swung her head from side to side, glaring and my heart quickened. Just then the calf struggled to its knees, rump in the air, and rose on its gangly legs. I barked, trying to warn Sally.

Startled, she turned and saw the calf and its mother. Stifling a scream, she crawled from the bushes and up the hill as fast as she could.

I barked again. My hair bristled, and I backed down the hill away from Sally in fear.

The moose leaped, her forelegs pawing the air. I darted away, the firewood banging my side, and ran

past the calf. The moose galloped after me, crushing the brush in her anger.

From the corner of my eye, I saw Sally scramble to her feet. Grabbing the bucket and satchel, she ran up the hill and disappeared over the side.

I raced on, trying to get away from the mama moose, blundering through brambles and flowers. The wood on my harness caught on branches and ripped from the straps.

Finally I could no longer hear the moose. Panting and tired, I slowed. When I looked back, she stood over her calf, lovingly cleaning it with her tongue.

Relief filled me. Now I had to find Sally. I trotted up the hill, giving the moose and her baby a wide berth. Dropping my head, I caught her scent, which zigzagged through the brush.

"Murphy." I heard a low call. She stood up from behind a hillock and waved urgently. I ran up to her, and she gave me a hug. I wagged my tail and whole rump with joy. "I'm so glad you're all right. Thank you for saving me. I didn't see the moose or her calf until you barked."

I licked her face, which was pale. Usually Sally was brave, so I was surprised to see her cheeks so white.

She took my head in her trembling hands. "I am so sorry I hit you. How could I have doubted you? It will never happen again. *I promise.* The boys in town were wrong, you aren't a scaredy-cat."

Only I was. I ran from the moose just as I had run from other dogs, the boys in town, and Carlick. But since it had chased me instead of Sally, she had been able to get away.

❧

"What happened to your dress, young lady?" Mama asked when we finally returned. She stood in front of a smoky fire outside our tent, and I could smell beans and beef simmering.

"My dress?" Sally echoed. Her white pinafore

was streaked with mud, and her flowered skirt was ripped where I had grabbed it. Before coming home, she had again picked up more sticks and tied them to my harness. But we had lost all the blueberries.

"Where is your bonnet, what are those things on your feet, and where have you *been?*" Mama's voice rose high and tight like the day she had given Sally a shake. I slunk to the other side of the fire, wanting to get away.

"I was fishing." Sally pulled the oilcloth-wrapped fish from her satchel. "And collecting wood. The driftwood on the beach is about gone. You needn't have worried. Murphy was with me."

Mama didn't even glance my way. For a long moment, she stared at Sally. When she did speak, her voice had dropped to almost a whisper. "Look at you, my lovely daughter. Your hair is tangled, and your skin is as brown as a native's. And instead of being a Gibson girl, I am a mess too. My one good dress has been ruined, and my fingers are sore from typing all day. Our house is filled with sand, and the sides flap and the roof leaks during storms. Grandmama was right. We never should have come to Nome."

"Grandmama was *not* right," Sally protested. "I love it here. Yes, it is wild and cold and we live in a tent. But the tundra is beautiful and you should have seen the blueberries. We would have brought you a bucketful, only the moose—"

Sally caught herself, but not before Mama heard her. Her face drained of color. Then slowly she turned away from her daughter, bent over the pot, and stirred. "Supper is ready," she said tightly. "I am not hungry and have typing to do before I retire." With sagging shoulders, she went into the tent.

Sally's lower lip quivered as she watched her mother go. "It's all right, Murphy." She untied my harness straps. "It's just that Mama works day and night. She's more tired than angry. She's right about the tent, though. We must find gold so we can buy a cabin. Come. Let's fry these fish. A good meal will make her feel better."

But a good meal didn't tempt Mama. Rapid

click-clacking came from the tent, and no amount of cajoling on Sally's part would persuade her mother to stop typing and come eat. Much to my delight, I got to eat a whole fish, plus part of Sally's, for now she wasn't hungry either.

When the frying pan had cooled, I licked up the last of the lard. Then Sally washed it with water and sand. By the time we had finished, the sun was lowering for the night.

When we returned to the tent, Mama stood outside with a creased piece of paper in her hand. "I have written to your grandparents, Sally," she said. "I have told them that we are booking passage on the *Lucky Lady* for home."

For an instant Sally was too stunned to speak. "Y-y-you mean leave Nome?" she stammered. "But Mama, we can't. I love it here."

"Tomorrow I am buying tickets. The steamship leaves August 7; that's in four days. We will arrive in Seattle by the end of August. We may miss your Grandfather's arrival here in Nome, which is unfortunate, but I will leave word for him. Grandmama will be triumphant that we have given up, but I will deal with her."

"Mama, no!" Sally cried out. "*This* is my home, not San Francisco."

I whined anxiously, hearing the emotion in their voices. Things had been so right since I met Sally and Mama. Now suddenly they were so wrong. And I didn't know how to help.

"It's done, and I will hear no more of it," Mama said. "Now pack a valise. We are going to the bathhouse to wash ourselves and our clothes. We may not be Gibson girls, but we needn't smell like beggars." She pointed the letter at me. "That goes for you too, Murphy," she added before disappearing into the tent.

I lowered my head at Mama's stern words. But when I glanced over at Sally, her eyes were narrowed and her lips were pressed firmly together.

As she stared after Mama, her fingers found my head. She stroked my ears just the way I liked and said in a low voice, "I believe our plans have changed, Murphy. We must stake our claim sooner than I thought. I am not leaving with Mama on the *Lucky Lady*. As soon as my gear is ready, we are off to the Snake River to find gold."

I understood the word "gold," but I did not know the rest of Sally's words. Still I shivered, sensing that what had just happened between Mama and Sally would forever change all our lives.

CHAPTER TEN

Up the River

August 7, 1900

Sally and I were ready to set out at midday, laden with supplies. My harness was heavy, packed with two rolled up oilcloths, netting, a rope, a scoop, a mining pan, a frying pan, and a lantern. Sally carried food, fishing gear, utensils, matches, candles, a wool blanket, *Grimm's Fairy Tales,* and clothing in a canvas pack on her back. She had mittens and jacket looped over her belt, as well as a knife in a sheath. Gone were her pinafore, bonnet, and boots. Instead she wore mukluks, leggings under her skirt, and a brimmed hat onto which she had sewn mosquito netting. Sally left a letter for Mama, and we headed up the beach.

Mama had not changed her mind about leaving Nome. In the last two days Sally had packed bit by bit in secret whenever Mama was at work, and each time I tried on my harness, it grew heavier and heavier.

We both banged and clattered as we walked to the dock that jutted into the Snake River where it met the Bering Sea. There, we climbed into a boat pulled by a team of four dogs. The dogs clambered along the riverbank, occasionally splashing in the water while a boatman stood in the bow, using a long pole to keep the hull in deeper water and away from the shore. There were many barrels and crates on the boat, but no other passengers.

"Where are you and your dog headed, miss?" the boatman asked after introducing himself as Mr. Lindblom. "You appear to be packed for a long trip."

"As far as we can go upriver," Sally said. "Where is your last stop?"

"Usually two miles inland," he told her. "That's where I drop the last supplies."

"I would like to pay you to go beyond that spot— as far as you can." She held several coins out to him.

Staring at the coins, Mr. Lindblom raised one brow. "Does your papa know you are out and about on your own?"

"Thank you for your concern." Sally sounded as grown-up as Mama. "I am heading upriver to my father's mining camp now. And I am not alone." She draped her arm over my neck. "I have Murphy."

"Your papa's beyond Point Crossing?" he asked.

Sally nodded. "Yes. It will be a hike from there, and my dog and I would be grateful for a boat ride as far as possible."

"We-l-l-l..." He scratched under his sweaty hat as he thought. "The river is high, but as soon as the bottom of the boat scrapes, I will have to let you off on shore."

"Thank you, sir."

For a few minutes the boat surged up the Snake,

with only the noise of the barking dogs filling the air. The shore was dotted with signs of miners—piles of rubble, rusting machines, broken pilings—but few men were working. Sally kept her arm around my neck. I leaned against her and felt her tremble. Was she as worried as I about this strange journey?

I began to pant. The day had warmed, and I was hot under my harness. As if Sally understood, she loosened the straps and let the harness fall to the bottom of the boat.

"Not many miners up the Snake," Mr. Lindblom said. "Most are on Anvil or Dexter Creeks where the richest placer claims have been found. Although McKenzie and Carlick have two large mines upriver. Your pa with them?"

"No, sir."

"That's good. Best to steer clear of anyone from Alaska Gold Mining Company. Heard there's trouble coming for that lawless crew."

Sally's arm tightened around me. "What kind of trouble?"

"Owners of Pioneer and Wild Goose Mining have hired lawyers to stop McKenzie, Carlick, and Judge Noyes from stealing claims. The law is slow, though, so in the meantime, that crooked bunch is gutting as many mines of gold as they can."

The boatman called to his dogs, and then added, "My uncle was one of the three Swedes to discover gold in the area."

"That's so interesting. Did he get rich?"

Lindblom snorted. "He left Nome poor. Judge Noyes changed the law, saying a foreigner couldn't file a proper claim. He evicted my uncle and other rightful owners and gave the claims to McKenzie and his bunch. The only gold I'll ever earn is ferrying the men who swindled my own kin."

As we approached a huge mine with machinery that rose into the sky, Mr. Lindblom shouted to his dogs to *whoa*. Pausing at a planked area on the shore, he dropped off several crates.

Two men came down to help. They stared at Sally. Quickly she turned her back on them. "Look,

Murphy," she whispered. "The sign says 'Alaska Gold Mining Company. No Trespassing.' This must be McKenzie and Carlick's mine."

Carlick. I had already heard that name too many times today.

"I did not dare file a claim in case Mama got wind of it," she continued in a low voice, "so we will try to travel far beyond any established mines. I do not want to encounter an angry prospector."

The boatman clicked, and the team started off again. I noticed how well he cared for his dogs. During the trip they had frequents rests, pats, and treats. Not all masters were like Carlick.

As we floated northward, signs of active mines disappeared, and we mostly passed piles of rusting and rotting equipment. We saw a small Native village of scattered tents, then a herd of elk, and then nothing but stretches of tundra. When we neared a spot where stunted pines drooped over the water, the boatman called to his dogs.

"Far as I can go, miss," he said, rapping the end

of the pole on the bottom of the river. "Rocks are ready to rip open my hull and the current is wearing out my team."

"Yes, sir!" Sally hurriedly reattached my harness, and I leaped from the boat, causing it to sway. "Thank you!"

Mr. Lindblom helped Sally off the boat. "Good luck on your journey, miss. I hope your father appreciates your effort." Then he pointed his finger at her. "And tell your father to stay away from McKenzie, Carlick, and his bunch."

"I will." Sally scrambled up the river bank, with me after her, and waved goodbye.

Mr. Lindblom whistled and called to his dogs as he turned them around. Sally and I watched the boat float quickly from sight, the current pushing them. Then suddenly it was silent except for the rustle of the river.

The tundra stretched in all directions without a house, tent, or tree rising into the sky. Wildflowers and grasses blew in the breeze. It was beautiful, vast, and quiet.

I sniffed the clean air. I was glad to be away from Nome and the clanking and crashing of the people, the machinery, and the sea. Beside me, I felt Sally shudder.

"It's just us now, Murphy," she whispered. "We are truly on our own."

Whining, I butted my head against her side. Was it worry I heard in her voice? Did she want to turn back?

Then she whooped excitedly. "Oh, Murphy, I have been waiting for this adventure since we arrived from San Francisco!" she exclaimed. "Come on, let's find our camp—and our gold!"

❦

We hiked through squishy bogs and over drier hillocks. Sometimes we followed a trail well worn by other prospectors and animals. Sometimes we slogged through thick mud and brush. Sally wore her mask of netting, but mosquitoes stung my nose until she greased it with lard.

We kept the river in sight, only leaving it twice when we heard voices. There were gold seekers even this far upland, and Sally was determined not to meet them and their nosy questions.

At one point the trail followed a ridge cut into the bank. Sally had to sidestep to keep from pitching over the small cliff, which sloped down to the river. I followed her, my claws scrabbling at the dirt to keep from sliding too. Once we had reached the other side, Sally let out a relieved breath. By then the sky was turning gray.

"Let's camp here tonight, Murphy." She dropped her pack to the ground and unstrapped my harness. I shook, glad to be rid of the burden.

We ate cold beans and biscuits for dinner. Then Sally wrapped herself in the blanket and oilcloth and promptly fell asleep. I lay down beside her, head perched on my paws, and kept watch.

The next day, we again hiked for miles. Finally Sally stopped at a bend in the river, where a brushy willow hung over a shallow, sandy pool. Firewood was scattered nearby, and weeds had started to grow again in what had been a cleared area. Someone must have camped here.

A breeze blew, scattering the mosquitoes. Behind us, ptarmigan sounded their throaty calls.

"What do you think, Murphy?" Sally asked.

I whacked my tail heartily, ready to stop.

"I think we're far enough away from Carlick and his crew. We'll camp here tonight and see if it suits."

After Sally took off my harness, I waded in the river. The water cooled my tired paws, and I drank greedily.

Sally waded in beside me, her feet bare. "Brrr! It's cold. Look!" she said. "Black sand under my toes. Surely we can find some gold in it. Perhaps the miner panning here before us is now living in a castle."

Giggling, she splashed me. I kicked up great

waves with my back legs, splashing her back. Then I saw a large flash of silver dart from under a rock. I lunged, catching a good-size salmon in my jaws. It twisted, but I kept hold. I was hungry.

"What a mighty hunter you are, Murphy!" Sally exclaimed. "If salmon and black sand are in this pool, it *will* be a good place to stay. I'll get a fire started."

As Sally gathered the wood strewn on the shore, she began to sing, the words filling the air with her happiness.

But as the sun dropped, my ears began to pick up the sounds of the night. Sally could not hear the distant howls, snorts, and yips, but I did. My journey from Dawson City had taught me that the land was filled with wolves, bear, and fox.

I *wasn't* a mighty hunter. But I hoped that I could keep Sally safe in the wilds of the tundra.

CHAPTER ELEVEN

Danger

August 16, 1900

Nine days of panning and not one nugget." Sally was knee-deep in water, tilting her pan back and forth and side to side. Her legs were bare, her skirt was caught up in her belt to keep it dry, and her hair was tucked under her hat. "A flake or two, yes, and flour, which is filling my vial. But if we are to buy a cabin, I need to find something bigger."

I stared into the water where it rippled over the rocks, intent on a different kind of prize—a silvery salmon. Hunger was always on my mind, even though I had caught several hares and a ptarmigan and found nests of birds' eggs and a lush gooseberry patch. I might not be courageous, but my stomach drove me to be a patient and crafty hunter for food.

Sally picked the pebbles out of the pan and tossed them in the river. Then she dipped the pan in the water again and began to shake and swirl the sand and gravel that remained. "Though I *am* getting better at this. It's good Mr. Smithson made me practice."

I cocked my head, listening—not to Sally's words, but to another sound in the distance: a rumble. A storm? So far, we'd been lucky—only light rain and fog that hadn't kept me from hunting or Sally from prospecting. Storms on the tundra could be fierce, but the sky was blue to the horizon.

"I've been keeping count of the days, Murphy. If Mama left with the ship, she should be halfway to Seattle. Do you think she did go?" Sally sounded anxious. "I wouldn't blame her for leaving me after what I did." She jutted her chin. "But I had no choice. I was not returning to San Francisco."

Sally dumped the sand in the pan back into

the river. "No gold. Not even a flake." She sighed. "Maybe when we get back to Nome, Grandpapa will be there. He said he was coming on business. What business, you ask?" She shrugged. "'A young girl does not speak of such things with an adult.'" She said in a Mama-like voice. "I say 'humph' to that."

Whap! A salmon flipped into the air and landed back in the water with a smack. I plunged my muzzle into the water, trying to catch it, but it slipped away.

Another rumble. This time when I lifted my head and sniffed, I could smell the rain in the air. Angry clouds had gathered in the north.

Sally and I had dug a burrow into the half-frozen bank, and she had fitted it with a roof and walls made of oilcloth to keep out the moisture. A veil of netting protected us the mosquitoes. Both of us slept tight as ticks in the hole. It had stood up to rain and the constant wind, but it hadn't been tested by a storm yet.

"If she's gone, you and I will still need a cabin." Sighing, she stood and rubbed her back. "Nome winters will be as fierce as Grandmama."

Then another sound reached my ears—the howl of wolves. We had heard them at night when we were safe in our burrow. I had also heard them on my trek from Dawson City to Nome. Old Blue had taught me that the pack howled before a hunt and after, but never during.

Ignoring the noises for now, I turned my attention to finding another salmon. A crash across the river startled me, and a lone buck leaped from the brush and into the water. He bounded toward us, spray flying skyward and making him look as if he had wings. He charged past so fast, I didn't even get off a *woof.*

Sally stared open-mouthed as the buck jumped over the stacked firewood and disappeared. "Did you see that? He was so beautiful—and not at all afraid of us."

I knew why he wasn't scared of us. The whites of his eyes and the foam flecking his mouth told me that he was running for his life. The wolves were after him.

Sally bent down and inspected her pan. "Murphy!" she gasped. "A nugget!"

I had no time for gold. If the deer was running from the wolves, the pack would be right behind him, following his trail right to Sally and me.

Whirling, I sprang toward Sally and barked furiously. I rammed her with my head, knocking her in the direction of the burrow. The pan flew from her grasp, plopping into the water. "Murphy!" she screeched. "You made me lose—" Then I saw understanding in her eyes.

Again I pushed her toward the burrow. She dove into the hole and pulled her knife from the sheath. I was prepared to stand guard, but she grabbed my collar and dragged me in after her. Then she yanked the tarp down in front of the entrance.

Wolves had never attacked our dog team or even come into camp when I was with Carlick. But there had always been fires and men with torches and rifles. I did not know what a pack would do if it caught Sally alone and in its path.

Moments later we heard the splashing of bodies and the drumming of paws. I could hear their panting and smell their scent. I shivered and Sally held me close. She was shivering too, but she bravely clasped the knife in front of her.

Then in a *whoosh,* as if they were a cloud blown by the wind, the wolves passed us.

We waited. "Do you think it's safe?" Sally

whispered. "Oh, it *must* be safe. I have to find that nugget before it gets swept away!"

Throwing back the tarp, she scrambled from the burrow and ran down to the river's edge. I trotted after her, glancing uneasily in the direction the wolves had gone. What if the deer doubled back and led them to us again?

"I was standing right there, wasn't I?" she asked, pointing to an eddy by some rocks. She had a fever in her gaze that reminded me of the buck.

"Or was it over there? Oh, there's the pan!" She snatched it from the water. "It's empty!" Dropping it, she dug furiously at the river bottom. "The nugget must be here somewhere."

I sat on the shore, straining to hear the wolves. The rumbling in the sky turned into a boom, the dark clouds drew overhead, and the wind began to flail the brush along the banks. A storm would soon be upon us. Sally was so intent on finding the lost nugget, she didn't seem to notice.

Suddenly, lightning zigzagged to the earth. It

struck so close that my fur crackled. Then the rain came, whipping the river with its gusting torrents.

"No-o-o!" Lifting her head, Sally howled, sounding like a wolf herself. Rain pelted her cheeks and dripped from her hat. Then her shoulders slumped as if she knew there was no use looking. Calling to me, she dragged herself to the burrow. Hurriedly I crawled in after her.

"It's lost, Murphy," she whispered as we huddled together, both of us drenched. "That nugget would have bought our cabin and a winter's stay. But now it's gone and all is lost."

I ran my tongue over Sally's wet cheek. But she stared straight ahead as if she didn't see me. "What if I have to leave Nome too? What if Grandpapa is in Nome and he makes me go back with him? Oh, Murphy, I can't go back to Grandmama's house. Even with you there, it will be intolerable. Lessons and corsets and unreasonable rules that *must be obeyed.*"

I could hear the despair in Sally's voice. We had

survived the wolves and now faced a storm. But she didn't seem to care. Whining deep in my throat, I wrapped myself around her, trying to keep us warm, and gently laid my head on her leg.

CHAPTER TWELVE

Lost

August 20, 1900

The storm continued for four days, pummeling the
tundra with wind, rain, and lightning. Sally and I
dined on canned beans and sardines, and we only left
the burrow to do our business. Even then, venturing
just three feet up the bank, the fear of being swept
away was real, and she held on to my collar as we
made our way behind a bush. Each time we returned
soaked, it took longer and longer to warm up.

Sometimes Sally shook with the cold. Her
clothes, my fur, and the lone blanket stayed damp.
The fire had long since died out. Fortunately the

burrow didn't collapse, though water leaked around the edges of the oilcloth and pooled by the entrance.

When there was enough light, Sally read to me from *Grimm's Fairy Tales*. "Hansel and Gretel" was her favorite story. She delighted in switching voices for each character, cackling hysterically when she was the witch.

"I would never be as silly as Hansel and drop bread crumbs to find my way," she scoffed. "You would gobble them up and so would the birds, and I would be as lost as Gretel."

Later, when it grew dark, Sally would fall into a restless sleep. That's when I grew alert. My ears stayed pricked for signs and sounds of danger. What if a bear found our buried food? The river might reach our hole. A wolverine could blunder into our burrow. Or a poisonous spider might crawl from behind the oilcloth.

Finally the storm blew itself out, and the sun rose hot and bright. We emerged like foxes from a lair and shook ourselves. Sally shed her wet clothes. She washed them in the river and draped them over the willow to dry. Then she gathered wood to make a fire.

I bounded up the bank and raced around the tundra, glad to stretch my legs. A ptarmigan burst into the air, and I set my sights on hunting. A diet of beans had left my stomach wanting.

I didn't like leaving Sally for long, but hunger drove me. Finally I brought back a hare. I held it high and proud as I trotted into camp. By then, Sally had a fire burning. The blanket and oilcloth, which she had also washed, hung on sticks to dry.

"Murphy, you are a wonder!" Taking the hare, she twisted a hind leg and began to pull off the hide. "I am glad Grandpapa taught me how to skin and cook a rabbit," she said. "We need fresh meat in our bellies. Oh, I miss him! I imagine he and Grandmama will be glad when Mama arrives home safely. Not that San Francisco is home to *me* anymore. I wonder if I will even be missed."

The roasting hare smelled delicious. Sally buried

several potatoes in the coals and I knew we would have a feast.

While we waited for the food to cook, Sally waded into the water. "I'm going to find that nugget, Murphy. Or one like it," she said, as she began to pan. "We missed four days due to the rain. August is coming to an end, and the storm was only a taste of winter. I know we must head back to Nome soon, but I won't leave until I have my prize."

Sally scooped sand and dirt from the river bottom into the pan. Then she dipped the pan into the water, swirling and shaking it, intently watching for gold. Finally I had to bark, reminding her that the hare was done.

She ate quickly, tossing me the bones, and then went back to work. In her zeal, she forgot to bury the rabbit hide away from our camp so it would not attract wild visitors. I dragged it far into the tundra and left it, stopping to eat some gooseberries on my way back.

A grunt made the hair on my back rise. I crouched

and peered from behind the scraggly bushes. A bear and her two cubs were dining on berries too. Their silver-tipped hides were glossy. The mama bear's claws were long and sharp as she stripped berries from the branches.

The cubs gamboled around their mother, who was as intent on berries as Sally was on gold. I did not dare run. But then the mother bear's nose began to twitch, and I knew she had smelled me. Nothing is fiercer than a mother grizzly guarding her cubs.

I flattened myself against the boggy earth, trying to disappear. She rose on her hind feet and looked around, huffing. I squeezed my eyes shut, wanting to disappear into the ground. Dropping to all fours, she began to lumber in the direction of the camp.

I couldn't let her find Sally. Leaping up, I barked, startling her. The cubs squealed as if hurt. With a clack of her teeth, the huge bear sprang toward me.

Grizzlies are fast, but not as fast as a frightened dog. I raced away from Sally and our camp, zigzagging from hillock to hillock. My paws, stabbed by thorns and scraped by roots, were raw and bloody.

When the mother bear charged after me, the babies followed, bawling because they couldn't keep up. When it seemed I could run no longer, the big grizzly stopped. Turning, she gathered her cubs and peacefully headed toward the horizon as if the encounter had never happened.

I dropped to my belly, panting wearily, until their silvery backs were out of sight. By then it was dark. I sat up and looked around. The tundra flowed around me like the sea. I had no sense where I was. Which way was the river?

Sight would not help me. I had to rely on my nose.

Dropping my head, I retraced my steps. The bears' scents wound to and fro, and I often had to stop and circle back. I feared for Sally, who'd never been alone at night. Not that I was a great protector. It seemed all I could do was run away.

I quickened my step, stopping only to find my trail or listen for the river. *Did I go in this direction before?* With the bear hot on my tail, I had run blindly.

The chilly wind made me shiver. The vast sameness of the tundra confused me. I caught my scent again and trotted off, suddenly realizing I was tracking back the way I had just come. Sitting on my haunches, I tipped back my head and bayed.

"Murphy!" Sally's voice was faint, but it was enough.

With renewed energy, I galloped toward the sound. A distant light glowed in the air.

"Murphy!"

I woofed, telling Sally I was coming. The light bobbed closer as if she was running too. With one last leap, I landed at her feet. She dropped her torch, which hissed in the bog.

"I thought you were gone forever!" She hugged me tightly against her. "What happened? Where were you?"

Lost, I wanted to tell Sally, but I could only wiggle and nuzzle her.

"It doesn't matter. Only you must never leave me again. *Nothing* is more important than you—

and Mama—I realize that now." Sally choked on her words, and I could hear the sob in her voice. "It doesn't matter if we don't find that nugget. Tomorrow we'll head back to Nome. If Mama's there, if she didn't leave for Seattle, I'll tell her how sorry I am—about leaving her and making her worry. Oh, I hope she will be there!"

Scrambling to her feet, Sally wrapped her fingers around my collar. Then she picked up the torch and held it in front of her. It shone on a piece of paper stuck on a thorn. "This way, Murphy. I marked my trail with pages from *Grimm's Fairy Tales* so I wouldn't get lost. I wasn't going to be as foolish as Hansel. Now let's go back and start packing. We'll leave in the morning."

I barked, ready to go home too. I'd had enough of wolves, mosquitoes, storms, bogs—and bears!

CHAPTER THIRTEEN

A Long Journey

August 21, 1900

We do have quite a bit of gold flour and flakes," Sally said as she tightened the harness around my chest. "It is safe in my silver vial. Perhaps Mr. and Mr. Hughes will take that as a first payment for the cabin. We can hope, can't we, Murphy?"

I sat on my haunches, resting before the long trek home. Sally darted around the camp like a blackfly. She couldn't stay still, and I worried she would wear herself out before we left.

"Let me clean the frying pan before I tie it to your harness." She glanced up at the sky. "Oh, clouds are gathering again! I hope we make it to Nome before another storm."

The wind whisked from the north, cutting through my fur, which was starting to thicken for the winter. Sally wore her leggings and jacket against the chill. I was glad we were leaving before the weather grew worse.

She gathered sand and used it to scrub the pan, which was greasy from the last of the bacon that she had cooked for our breakfast. "Do you think our tent is still waiting on the Nome beach?" Peering back at me, she wrinkled her nose. "Though after camping in the quiet of the tundra, I do not wish to live there again. That's another reason we need a cabin. The Hughes home is far enough from town to be peaceful, but near enough to walk to Front Street even in four feet of snow."

She dipped the pan in the river to rinse it, then froze. Frowning, she stooped and peered into the water. Then she gasped, dropped the frying pan, and slowly reached her hand into the water. When she withdrew it, something glistened from between her thumb and finger.

"Murphy," she whispered. "It's the nugget. I found it!" Whooping, she sprang into the air, keeping her fist wrapped tight around the gold. She opened her hand. "Look at it! It's the size of a coin! Oh, I won't lose it this time."

Yanking at the leather strap around her neck, she drew the vial from her bodice. Then she looked over at me. "I know a better place to keep this safe." She found the pocket on the inside of my canvas collar and tucked the nugget inside. It felt like a knot at my neck. "You are the only one I trust, Murphy."

Something wet plopped on my nose. A snowflake. Tipping back my head, I looked skyward. The clouds were thick and low.

"Snow in August. Ugh. Come on, Murphy. It's time to go." Sally stood and surveyed the camp where we'd spent the past weeks. Then, hitching her pack securely on her shoulders, she strode off.

Snow began to fall harder as we trudged

downriver, keeping the water in sight as best as we could. We followed a deer path that meandered along one side, until it curved inland. By then I was making deep tracks in the snow. We had to stop often to shake off Sally's mukluks and pull ice balls from my paws.

When the snow got too thick and the sky too dark to see, Sally stopped under a tangle of willow roots. It was clear underneath and gave some protection from the wind. She unhooked my harness, which dropped to the ground with a clang of supplies. Then she pulled the blanket from her pack and wrapped it around herself. She opened a can of beef and shared it with me. I was weary, and I could tell Sally was just as tired. Draping the oilcloth on top of the roots, she crawled underneath. "Come on, Murphy." She gestured for me to join her, but I scooted away. I needed to keep lookout. Sleep for me would not be easy. Snow did not keep Alaskan creatures from hunting.

I dozed fitfully until the sky turned from black to gray. It was still snowing, and a small drift kept us snug under the roots until Sally woke up. Breakfast was a bit of dried beef and the last of the biscuits, which were as hard as stones. My mouth watered for a juicy salmon.

"Nome should be one or two more days' trek," Sally said as she packed up her gear and tied on my harness. "Hunger will make us walk faster."

But when we crawled from the hole, we realized that the snow was much deeper now. It reached the top of Sally's mukluks and almost touched my belly. It was wet and heavy, making our journey slow and hard.

Sally tried to stay next to the river, where the heat from the rushing water had melted some of the snow. But it was slippery, and after falling twice, she gave up and climbed back to the flat tundra.

When we reached the high bank where the trail cut into the ridge, Sally cheered. "This is where we camped the first night. We are halfway home!" Then her face fell. "Not quite. I forgot that Mr. Lindblom ferried us farther up the river. We'll have to make it

to Point Crossing before we can catch the boat." She sighed wearily. "At least it is not too cold."

Reaching into her pack, she pulled out the beef and a few dried apricots. "This will be our lunch and dinner." We ate standing, fat flakes settling on her shoulders and hat and on my back. I shook, but the snow was so wet that it stuck. Sally ran her hand along my spine to clear it. Then she took off her hat and banged it against her leg.

"We'll have to carefully make our way along this path," she said. "The snow's packed on the ridge that hangs over the trail. And there's a steep drop to the river." She shivered as she glanced down to the rushing water. It would be slippery too.

Sally went first, placing one foot carefully in front of the other. The flakes fell so fast and heavy that I could barely see her. Then above us, I heard a rumble. I barked. Sally turned and looked at me, then up at the overhang. Under the brim of her hat, I saw fear in her eyes as the rumble turned to a roar. The overhang, heavy with wet snow, gave way. It crashed over Sally, and she vanished in a cloud of white.

For an instant, I stood frozen in horror. The snow and Sally tumbled down toward the river in a swirl of mud and rock, and it landed in a huge mound. Without hesitating I leaped to the riverbank. Furiously I began to dig.

Somewhere in the icy pile, Sally was buried—and I had to get her out!

CHAPTER FOURTEEN

Desperation!

August 21, 1900

Snow and mud flew from beneath my paws as I dug, desperately trying to get to Sally. I barked, hoping she could hear me. I plowed into the mound with my muzzle, smelling for her. When I scented her jacket and felt her warmth, I dug even harder. Finally, I found her arm.

Grabbing her sleeve, I yanked, pulling until I could get a grip on the shoulder of her jacket. I tugged with all my might, until I could see her head.

I licked Sally's face clear of snow. Her eyes fluttered, and she tried to struggle upright. Her legs were still buried, and I clawed at the snow packed around them, careful not to scratch her. Once they were uncovered, I barked encouragement.

Sally's lips were blue. She needed to move to get warm again. Holding on to me, she tried to stand. She winced when she put weight on one leg. "I fear I twisted my ankle, Murphy. I need to make a splint. Grandpapa showed me how to fashion one like he had to during the war."

She took off her belt and slid off the sheath, the knife still in it. She secured the sheath to her ankle with her belt to create a splint. "This will have to do," she said grimly.

I stood next to her and she leaned on me to rise. "We have to get to Point Crossing and the mining camp before nightfall," she told me. "Thank the Lord the snow has stopped. That at least is in our favor."

Using me as a crutch, Sally hobbled along the river until we found a gentle rise up the bank. There we found a path trampled by animals and followed it. The sun peeked through the clouds. It warmed us, but also made the snow sticky like the oatmeal I used to lick from Mama's bowl.

Half walking, half hopping, and always leaning on me, Sally made her way. I could feel the exhaustion in her grip on my shoulder. I was tired too. And hungry. I did not know how far we had to go to reach Point Crossing. Before, we had traveled easily by boat. Plowing through thick snow was slow going. Could we make it by nightfall?

Suddenly, Sally slumped down on a small hillock. Her cheeks were white. Undoing the belt, she rubbed her ankle. It was swollen under her legging. "I can't go any farther, Murphy," she said. "Point Crossing is at least two more miles. Only I can't move another inch. My leg hurts so, and slogging through the snow is like walking in mush. Tomorrow, we can go on."

I pranced in front of her, whining, willing her to try. The feeble sun was dipping behind the horizon, the air growing sharp with cold. Sally's clothes were wet from her fall into the river. They would freeze stiff overnight. I didn't think she could survive outside with no fire.

Pulling off her pack, she removed the blanket and oilcloth and wrapped herself in them. Then she slid down in the protection of the hillock, curled in a ball, and shut her eyes.

I barked, but she didn't move. Frantic, I raced around her. *I had to do something!* I couldn't build a fire. I couldn't drag her two miles.

I could drape myself over her to keep her warm until morning. Or I could go to Point Crossing and summon help.

I hated to leave Sally, but I knew this was what I needed to do. I would run as fast as a deer in the snow. I would get to Point Crossing before nightfall and bring rescuers back to Sally.

I knew which way to go. The river guided me, and without Sally, I moved swiftly. Before long, I smelled smoke.

By the time I saw the glow of the campfire, the sky was dark. I bounded into a circle of men sitting on crates around a fire and eating from metal plates. Two of them sprang up and reached for rifles. Another held up a lantern.

For a second, I was blinded by the brightness. Fear coursed through me as I remembered the gang of men chasing me down the street in Nome. My legs wanted to turn and run, but I thought of Sally.

"What in tarnation is that?" one of the men exclaimed.

I barked and whirled in the direction I had come.

"Put down your rifles, you idiots," a deep voice said. "It's a dog."

"A mighty *big* dog," another added.

A tall man rose from his seat on a crate. "Looks like he's wearing a pack. Must be a miner's dog."

"Boss said he'd heard rumors someone was panning at the bend."

I barked again. The tall man stepped closer but I darted out of reach. I looked over my shoulder and whined. *Follow me. Follow me.*

"If it's a miner's dog, where's the miner?"

"The beast wants us to go with him," the tall man said. "Could be the miner's injured, and the dog's asking for help. Ford, Jones: grab your snowshoes and come with me."

"We worked like mules all day," one of the men grumbled. "If a man's foolish enough to be out in this snow and cold, he deserves to die."

This way! This way! I barked and barked until the tall man again gestured to two others. "That's an order. Let's see what this fool dog wants. If it's a miner, Carlick might give us a reward for putting a bullet in his head."

"Or might be the dog'll lead us to a steak dinner," another said with a chuckle.

With the three men following me, I trotted down the path away from the fire. They carried lanterns and rifles. But since they wore snowshoes and I had already carved a trail, we made fast time.

The moon had risen, so I could see the dark lump that was Sally. Whining, I nosed her and then woofed at the men: *Hurry! Hurry!*

The tall man bent over and shook Sally's shoulder. "Hey, wake up." When there was no response, he peeled back the oilcloth from around her head. "Why, it's a youngun'," he said. Shrugging off his coat, he wrapped it around her. "Kid's alive. Warm, actually. Let's get him back to camp." He bent to pick her up.

As he started to lift her, Sally awoke and began to struggle. "Who are you? What are you doing? Put me down!"

"What in the world?" He lifted his lantern higher. "It's a girl!"

"A feisty one."

"Calm down, miss," the tall man said. "I'm Jacob Beamer. We're from the Alaska Gold Mining Company at Point Crossing. Your dog came into camp and wouldn't leave us alone until we followed him."

"Lucky he did," the second man added, "or you'd be a grizzly dinner."

Sally's eyes shifted to me. I wagged my tail and lifted my lip in a smile of relief. She smiled back.

"We need to get you to our fire," Mr. Beamer said. "Can you walk?"

"My ankle is twisted."

"I'll carry you then. Grab her gear," he told one of the men as he hoisted Sally in his arms.

They all headed down the trail. Sally's head nodded against Mr. Beamer's shoulder.

When we reached the camp, he set her on a rock near the fire. She leaned forward and warmed her hands. Then she unhooked my harness so I could rest too.

I hugged her side, my gaze anxious. The men had saved Sally, yet they did not seem friendly.

"I'll get the boss," one of them said. He hurried over to a log cabin.

Mr. Beamer handed Sally a steaming mug of coffee and a plate of beef and beans. She took them with a gracious "thank-you," but I could see the wariness in her own eyes as she ate. When she was half-finished she set the plate in front of me so I could lap up the rest.

"I appreciate your help and the hearty meal, sir," Sally said. "Do you know when Mr. Lindblom will be arriving?"

"Midday tomorrow as always," he replied. "Are you going to tell us what you were doing on the tundra in the middle of a storm?"

"I'll tell you what she was doing!" A man strode toward us. "She was trespassing on *my* land and panning *my* gold."

My hair bristled. I knew who it was even before the flames lighted his face. *Carlick.*

A growl rose in my throat. Sally clutched my collar as Carlick marched up to us. Crossing his arms, he glared down at her.

"Right, little missy? You must be the one who's been mining the bend upriver. We heard rumors and sometimes smelled smoke. Did you know that land belongs to my company? Which means any gold you found belongs to me."

Sally's face paled, and she set down the coffee mug. Her eyes darted around the campfire as if hoping for an ally. But suddenly the other miners were looking away, finishing a meal, or cleaning equipment. Only Mr. Beamer appeared to be listening.

"The law says that's trespassing and stealing," Carlick went on. "We need to take her into town and have her arrested."

But Carlick didn't know Sally. My mistress had smudged cheeks, sodden clothes, and brush sticking out of her hair. Still, she slowly stood up in front of him, trying not to wince when she put weight on her sore leg. I stood too, ready to flee. I knew the meanness in Carlick. Sally didn't.

Tipping up her chin, she studied Carlick with a clear gaze. "And who are *you*, sir, to be issuing such threats?"

"Mr. Ruston Carlick, at your service." He grinned smugly. "Half owner of Alaskan Gold Mining Company, which has claimed the Snake River from Nome all the way to heaven."

"Oh, then you definitely don't own that bend;

that camp might be described as purgatory, but never as heaven."

Several men chuckled, and Carlick shot them warning looks.

Stooping, Sally picked up her pack and mine. "I thank your men for carrying me to the fire, fixing me a meal, and letting me warm myself, but my dog and I will be on our way."

Carlick's grin vanished. "Wrong, miss. You will not be on your way until you give me any gold you panned from that claim."

Sally's brow furrowed. I nudged her side, wanting her to give the man what he wanted so we could be gone.

"No, sir. I will not," she said. "I have heard of your reputation. You and McKenzie may have evicted the rightful owners from their claims with the help of Judge Noyes. You may have stolen gold from half the prospectors in Nome. But you will *not* take my hard-earned gains."

Throwing back his head, Carlick laughed uproariously. Then in one swift movement, he slapped Sally across the cheek, sending her sprawling sideways.

Anger coursed through me. I had run from Carlick and men like him all my life. But none of them had ever hurt Sally.

Carlick reached down to yank her up. Baring my teeth, I leaped, my jaws clamping on his outstretched arm.

CHAPTER FIFTEEN

Rescue

August 21, 1900

The force of my hurtling body sent Carlick flying backwards. He flailed at me with his other arm, but I hung on tight. My teeth gripped his wool coat, not flesh. Clamping down harder, I tasted blood. He bellowed like an elk. Suddenly men were upon me, beating me with sticks and rifle butts.

"No, Murphy! Stop! Let him go before they kill you!" Sally threw herself on top of me, receiving several blows on her back.

"Quit! All of you!" Mr. Beamer knocked the men out of the way.

Grabbing my collar, Sally pulled me from Carlick. I let go of his arm, but I couldn't stop snarling. I was filled with hatred.

Two men helped Carlick to his feet. His face was red with anger as he clasped his arm. "Murphy? That dog is *Murphy*?" Carlick spat out the words, as furious as I. "Grab him!" He reached under his coat and tore off his belt. "Muzzle him!"

The men pushed Sally out of the way. She pummeled them with her fists, and one man had to hold her back. It took four of them to muzzle me, and before they tightened the belt around my jaw, I drew blood on all of them.

"So this is Murphy." Carlick narrowed his eyes as he swung around to Sally. "Then it appears, little lady, that you have stolen more than gold from me. You have stolen my dog."

"He is *my* dog!" Sally retorted as she struggled futilely against the man holding her.

"We'll see about that." Carlick reached for my neck. I growled, and the men had to put all their weight on my back to hold me down. His fingers spread my fur by my shoulder. "Ha! Just as I thought. There is my *C* branded in his flesh. Proof that he is my dog, and *you* are a thief."

"Murphy will never be your dog," Sally snapped. "Here, take my gold." Wresting her arms from the man's grasp, she drew the silver vial from around her neck and threw it at Carlick. "It will pay for him."

With raised brows, he opened the vial and tapped the gold into his palm. "This? This is what you panned from the Snake?" He snorted. "This isn't enough to keep you out of jail, much less pay for the dog. He stays with me. I'll need a strong sled dog this winter. But right now I need to teach him who's the boss around here. Ford!" he shouted. "Get me my whip."

"No!" Dropping beside me, Sally reached under my collar and dug out the gold nugget. *"This* will pay for Murphy." She held it up. It gleamed in the firelight and Carlick's eyes grew bright with greed.

"Lord, that's the biggest nugget I've seen!" one of the men gasped.

Carlick took the nugget between his fingers and studied it before tucking it in his own pocket. "Well, well. You *were* lucky. This is probably worth hundreds of dollars. Which is a shame, since you found it on Alaska Gold Mining land. That means the dog is still mine, and you are still a thief."

Ford handed him the whip. Beside me, Sally stared up at him, defiant. "Then you will have to whip us both."

"Perhaps I will," he said, snapping the lash.

I rose suddenly to my full height, shaking off the men that held me. A roar rumbled in my throat. I lunged at the men, and they scattered like scared sheep. Then I faced Carlick.

Even with my jaw strapped shut, I was ready to fight the person I hated. I was ready to protect Sally.

Two men stepped from the shadows and flanked Carlick. One had a white beard. The other was younger with a dark mustache. And both had drawn their guns.

I could knock down Carlick. I might even dislodge the belt around my jaw and get in a bite. But I couldn't defeat a gun. I had seen one bullet fell a full-grown elk.

Still, I crouched, gathering my strength, ready to attack. I was willing to die protecting Sally.

Carlick raised the whip, but the white-bearded man caught his wrist before he could lash out.

"I wouldn't do that, sir," the older man said, yanking the whip from Carlick's grasp. The other man deftly pulled a gun from under Carlick's coat while aiming his own weapon in the direction of the other men. Arms in the air, the others backed off—except for Mr. Beamer, who came up beside the bearded man.

Sally gasped. "Grandpapa!" Launching herself in the air, she flung herself into his arms. "You came for me!"

"*Sally?*" the bearded man exclaimed. "What are you doing here?"

Dazed, I sank to the ground. Sally knelt beside me and took off the muzzle. "Oh, Murphy. Are you all right?"

I whined and stood, my eyes still on Carlick. But he was no longer paying attention to me. "Who are you and what right do you have to burst into my camp and disarm me?" he demanded.

Sally's Grandpapa faced Carlick. "I am Judge William Morrow of the Ninth Circuit Court of Appeals. This is Deputy Marshall Harmon Frank. We traveled to Nome to see firsthand the gross abuse of power that the Alaskan Gold Mining Company— consisting of you, McKenzie, and Judge Noyes—has wielded over Nome."

"It is all legal!" Carlick bellowed. "You can ask Judge Noyes."

"We intend to." He pulled out a piece of paper from inside his pocket. "The circuit court has ordered that you and McKenzie are no longer the receivers of any claims. They will revert to their rightful owners."

"Nobody can take away our claims," Carlick scoffed. "McKenzie has many powerful friends in Washington, D.C."

Judge Morrow cut his eyes to Mr. Beamer. "Fortunately we had a man inside your camp who has witnessed you beating and threatening miners reluctant to abandon their claims. His testimony will land you in jail long enough for Washington to learn the truth. And long enough for us to prosecute McKenzie. Frank, tie his hands tightly."

"Beamer, you traitor!" Carlick lunged at the tall man, but the Deputy Marshall caught him and secured his hands.

"I'll take this into possession of the courts," Sally's Grandpapa said. He reached into Carlick's pocket and plucked out the nugget.

"That belongs to me!" Carlick sputtered.

"The court will decide," the Deputy Marshall said.

My head swung back and forth as I watched the men argue. Their words flew past me, but I did not care. Sally was safe, which was all that mattered. She kneeled beside me, her hand on my collar, until Beamer and the second man took Carlick away. Then her grandfather stooped beside us.

His eyes were grave. "You have much to explain, young lady. Your mama has been sick with worry."

"Mama is still in Nome?" Sally exclaimed.

"Of course. She would never leave you. Luckily I was on my way to Nome with the matters of the circuit court. When I arrived, I found her distraught. We searched everywhere for you, never realizing you would travel this far. Why on earth did you go off on your own?"

"To find gold, to buy a cabin for Mama, so we could stay the winter," Sally explained. "She threatened to leave Nome, only I'm not going back to San Francisco. I love it here. Besides, I wasn't on my own. I was with Murphy."

Grandpapa shook his head in wonder. "The only thing that kept your mama sane was that she knew you were with Murphy. She swore that he would keep you safe." Smiling, he stroked my head. "And from what I saw tonight, she was correct. Thank you, Murphy, for keeping my adventurous and foolish granddaughter from harm's way." Standing, he lifted Sally to her feet.

She stepped on her bad ankle and made a face.

"Are you all right?" he asked.

"A slight sprain. From the avalanche."

His face grew as white as his beard. "Avalanche?"

"Don't worry, Murphy dug me out. I had my knife and made a splint as you taught me. And really, it was nothing compared to the storm and the wolves."

"Storm? Wolves?" Grandpapa's eyes grew wider. "I want to hear the whole story, young lady, but now we must be on our way. There are several boats waiting for us at the dock. I'll have Beamer bring your packs. You may tell me these hair-raising tales as we travel back to Nome. But then we will not speak of them again. We will tell your mother that you stayed with a friendly miner and his family."

"That would be lying, Grandpapa," Sally said.

"It would also be sparing your mother's heart."

"Oh, Mama is not as weak as you think." Using me and her grandfather as supports, Sally began to hobble down to the dock. "Grandpapa, what about my gold nugget?"

He sighed. "At this point, it belongs to the courts until the matter of the Alaska Gold Mining Company is settled."

"But how will I buy a cabin for Mama?"

"I will be staying in Nome until McKenzie and Carlick are prosecuted. That may take all winter. Perhaps there is a comfortable home that a judge could afford?"

Sally grinned. "Perhaps." Then her smile faded. "And Murphy?" she asked in a small voice as she laced her fingers in my fur. "Carlick had him branded with his *C*. Will the courts uphold his ownership?"

Gravely he shook his head. "I don't know, Sally."

She stopped in her tracks. "Then I am not going back. Murphy and I will run away. We proved we could survive on the tundra. I would rather live like a wild fox than live without Murphy."

Grandpapa rolled his eyes. "You are such a stubborn child. Quite like your Grandmama. So you will not return to Nome unless Murphy is yours?"

"Correct."

"I guess it could be argued that you have been caring for Murphy for months."

"And add that Carlick was a cruel owner," Sally chimed in.

Grandpapa nodded in agreement. "Then by the power of the Circuit Court of San Francisco, I do deem that Murphy, your protector, as well as gold mining and pack dog of Nome, belongs to you, Sally Ann Dawson. Is that good enough?"

She shook her head. "I want it in writing with your official seal. Mama will type it up. She loves Murphy as much as I do."

"And my official seal will do?"

She nodded.

"All right then. Let's go back to Nome and your mama and get it done."

"Thank you, sir! One minute, please." Sally kneeled beside me. Tears suddenly streamed down her cheeks. Since I first met Sally on the beach, I had never seen her cry. I licked the tears from her face, wondering why she was crying now.

"This time it is really true, Murphy," she said. "Grandpapa has the power to make it so that Carlick can never take you away from me again."

I did not know Sally's words, but I knew by her

hug that she was happy despite her tears. I whapped my tail from side to side, as happy as she.

"Mama is waiting for us. We won't have to leave Nome. Isn't that the best news?"

Yes! I woofed.

"Come on. Let's go home." Sally stood. With one hand she held my collar. With the other she held her grandfather's hand, and together we walked to the boat.

My journey to Nome had started with Carlick. It had ended with Sally. Along the way, I had proven my bravery and helped save Sally, and now I knew that nothing—not moose, bear, storms, wolves, avalanches, or Carlick—could ever separate us.

Because finally I belonged to Sally.

And she belonged to me.

The History Behind *Murphy*

Dogs in Alaska

In the late 1800s and early 1900s, gold strikes in Alaska brought a rush of miners and opportunists. Big dogs like Murphy were used for hauling, transportation, companionship, and protection. In fact, they became more valuable than horses. "A dog that sold for fifteen dollars in Washington State would bring ten times that in the Yukon" (Murphy, *Gold Rush Dogs,* page 16).

Even before the gold rush, native Indians and Eskimos relied on dogs to transport their goods when they moved to and from their seasonal camping and hunting grounds. Inupiaq Eskimos made sleds of driftwood with bone runners and harnesses made of strips of moose and bearskin.

Dogsled teams were important, but so was the "one-man dog" like Murphy. Alaskans considered their dogs "worth their weight in gold." A prospector needed his dog for survival. All breeds of dogs were valued, from spaniels to huskies, but they had to be hardy and strong to withstand the harsh environment.

Cool Dogs

☞ Ella Fitz hid her money in a leather pouch on the collar of her dog Faust.

☞ Bill Skagway, buried in an avalanche, was rescued by his dog Yukon.

☞ Togo and Balto led dogsled teams to bring diphtheria serum to Nome.

The Nome Gold Rush

The town of Nome, isolated on the Bering Peninsula, relied on dog teams because it was iced in all winter. "All dog teams lead to Nome," said an Alaskan musher about the importance of dogsleds (Henning, *Nome: City of the Golden Beaches,* page 127). This was especially true during the gold rush that began in the spring of 1899 and ended in September 1900, when it seemed everyone was headed to Nome.

In 1899, gold was discovered in the sand of Nome's beaches and river bottoms. By 1900, the cry of "gold!" brought chaos to the area. News traveled to the states: there was "Gold in the creeks, gold in the beaches. Even the sands of the seashore gleamed with yellow flakes!" (Kunkel, *Alaska Gold: Life on the New Frontier, 1898–1906,* page 2). Prospectors looking for great wealth came by boat from the west coast as well as by dogsled, horse, bicycle, and on foot from other parts of Alaska.

These fortune hunters were called "sourdoughs" because many brought with them crocks of sourdough starter to use for biscuits. They were also referred to as "stampeders" since they raced to Nome once they heard the cry of "gold!" The town of Nome quickly swelled from a few thousand people to a population of 20,000.

By the end of the summer of 1900, the gold rush had ended and most people had left. The beach looked like a giant junkyard. Abandoned pumps, pipes, steam engines, tents, and rockers lined the shore. The "rotting timbers and rusting iron will only be left to tell the tale..." of many miners' lost dreams (Henning, *Nome: City of the Golden Beaches,* page 91).

Finding Gold

The stampeders and sourdoughs arrived in Nome hoping to strike it rich. But few made a fortune.

Panning for gold is an art, and most adventurers came unprepared both in knowledge and supplies. L. H. French, a mine manager, wrote in the *Nome Nugget* that miners "arrived on the gold fields without a dollar to their pockets or a penny's worth of supplies..." (Kunkel, *Alaska Gold: Life on the New Frontier, 1898–1906,* page 5).

In 1900, there were as many ways to mine as there were creative miners. Beginners like Sally mined by hand using a pan or a rocker, a device that looked like a cradle. Sluice boxes—long wooden channels—were also used by men such as Mr. Smithson. Seawater was poured down the sluice. The gold—heavier than water—sank and was caught in the riffles or grooves on the bottom of the box.

More elaborate contraptions were brought from the states. "At least 35 different kinds of patent gold saving devices and gold washing machines were on sale in Seattle" (Henning, *Nome: City of the Golden Beaches,* page 46). They were given names like Yoho's

Scientific Gold Trap and were guaranteed to work perfectly.

The Real Carlick

Finding gold was difficult, but so was hanging on to a claim. Claim jumpers—people who illegally took over others' mining areas—were a huge problem.

Carlick is fictional. But McKenzie, Judge Noyes, and the scandal involving the Alaska Gold Mining Company are real.

In the summer of 1900, McKenzie (the president of the Alaska Gold Mining Company) took over many of the richest claims in Nome. First he got his friend Judge Noyes, the new judge of the Second Judicial Division of Alaska (which included Nome), to evict the real owners. Then he moved in his own men and quickly stripped the mines of their gold. Meanwhile, Judge Noyes used the law to keep the real owners from taking back their claims. Because the judge was the highest authority in Nome, this illegal setup continued for several months. In August 1900, the lawyers for the other major mine companies went to San Francisco to seek justice. Still, McKenzie refused to obey. In October he was finally arrested.

Life in Nome

Sally and Mama arrived in Nome in the spring, when people could travel to the area. Most of the year Nome was locked in by ice and snow, and ships with supplies and news from the mainland could not reach the town. In the fall and winter Nome received only four hours of daylight. "We are prisoners in a jail of ice and snow," one newspaperman wrote in November 1900 (Henning, *Nome: City of the Golden Beaches,* page 122).

Even spring and summer could bring bad storms and 75 mph winds. The ground was frozen all winter. When it thawed, it turned roads and paths into rivers of mud two feet deep, making travel by land difficult.

In the summer there were sweltering 100-degree days that could drop to freezing temperatures at night. In July 1899, Ed McDaniel wrote of Alaska: "It is awfully hard to live up here. The mosquitoes are thick as bees and it rains all the time and the sun never sets. The ground is covered with moss and water" (Kunkel, *Alaska Gold: Life on the New Frontier, 1898–1906,* page 55).

In 1900, Nome was a rough place for women and children. In the beginning, there was no police force. The lure of gold brought swindlers, tinhorn gamblers, and con men. Front Street, which stretched for five miles, was lined with more saloons than stores. Gangs roamed the street, and as Sally mentions—but didn't include in her letter to Grandpapa—there were many murders.

Nome Today

Today in Nome the weather is still unpredictable. As always, the summer days are long and the winter days are short. The town has a population of over 3,000, and it is still one of the most remote communities in Alaska. And gold is still being mined. In fact, Nome is experiencing a second gold rush.

With the price of gold rising, Nome has become a hot destination. In January 2013, *ABC News* reported that gold fever was again gripping adventurers looking for riches. The Discovery Channel's reality television show *Bering Sea Gold* features miners dredging for gold in the bottom of the Bering Sea. Like the stampeders of the first gold rush, these modern day prospectors are trying to hit it big. And like the prospectors of 1900, they still face incredible odds.

Bibliography

Henning, Robert A, Terence Cole and Jim Walsh. *Nome: City of the Golden Beaches.* Anchorage: The Alaska Geographic Society, 1984.

Jones, Preston. *Empire's Edge: American Society in Nome, Alaska, 1898–1934.* Fairbanks: University of Alaska Press, 2007.

Kunkel, Jeff, ed. *Alaska Gold: Life on the New Frontier, 1898–1906.* San Francisco: Scottwell Associates, 1997.

Murphy, Claire Rudolph and Jane G. Haigh. *Gold Rush Dogs.* Anchorage: Alaska Northwest Books, 2001.

Murphy, Claire Rudolph and Jane G. Haigh. *Gold Rush Women.* Anchorage: Alaska Northwest Books, 2003.

For Further Reading

DeClements, Barthe. *The Bite of the Gold Bug: A Story of the Alaskan Gold Rush.* New York: Viking, 1992.

Murphy, Claire Rudolph and Jane G. Haigh. *Children of the Gold Rush.* Boulder, CO: Roberts Rinehart Publishers, 1999.

Ransom, Candace. *Gold in the Hills: A Tale of the Klondike Gold Rush.* Renton, WA: Mirrorstone, 2008.

About the Author

When Alison Hart was seven years old, she wrote, illustrated, and self-published a book called *The Wild Dog*. Since then, she's authored more than twenty books for young readers, including *Darling, Mercy Dog of World War I; Finder, Coal Mine Dog; Leo, Dog of the Sea; Anna's Blizzard; Emma's River;* and the *Racing to Freedom* trilogy. She lives in Virginia.

www.alisonhartbooks.com

About the Illustrator

Michael G. Montgomery creates illustrations for advertising, magazines and posters, and children's books, including *Darling, Mercy Dog of World War I; Finder, Coal Mine Dog; Leo, Dog of the Sea; First Dog Fala;* and *Night Rabbits*. He lives in Georgia with his family and two dogs.

www.michaelgmontgomery.com

Also in the Dog Chronicles series

Darling, Mercy Dog of World War I
HC: 978-1-56145-705-2
PB: 978-1-56145-981-0

When the British military asks families to volunteer their dogs to help the war effort, Darling is sent off to be trained as a mercy dog. She helps locate injured soldiers on the battlefield, despite gunfire, poisonous gases, and other dangers. She is skilled at her job, but surrounded by danger. Will she ever make it back home to England?

"While never shying away from the tragedies of battle, Darling's story focuses on bravery, sacrifice and devotion... Wartime adventure with plenty of heart."
—*Kirkus Reviews*

Finder, Coal Mine Dog
HC: 978-1-56145-860-8

When Thomas's family needs money, he's forced to go to work in the coal mines, even though neither of his late parents wanted that for him. His only comfort is his dog Finder, a failed hunting dog who now pulls a cart in the mines. When disaster strikes, can Thomas and Finder escape from the fires deep below ground?

"Well-told and entertaining..." —*Kirkus Reviews*

❖ NCSS / CBC Notable Social Studies Trade Books for Young People

Leo, Dog of the Sea

HC: $12.95 / 978-1-56145-964-3

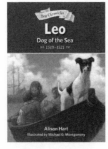

After three ocean voyages, Leo knows not to trust anyone but himself. But when he sets sail with Magellan on a journey to find a westward route to the Spice Islands, he develops new friendships with Magellan's scribe, Pigafetta, and Marco, his page. Together, the three of them experience hunger and thirst, storms and doldrums, and mutinies and hostile, violent encounters. Will they ever find safe passage?

★ "Frank history, attention to factual detail, and vivid adventures make this a standout." —*Kirkus Reviews*